GW00859236

Benny and Bobby Versus Adolf

How Two Lab Mice Took on an Evil

Empire

by Monica Porter

Benny and Bobby Versus Adolf
How Two Lab Mice Took on an Evil Empire
ISBN: 978-1-913781-21-7
Published by CAAB Publishing Ltd (Reg no 12484492)

C . A . A . B
PUBLISHING

Serenity House, Foxbridge drive, Chichester, UK
www.caabpublishing.co.uk

First Published 2022

1 3 5 7 9 10 8 6 4 2

Printed in the UK
British Library Cataloguing in Publication data available

To those who feel small and insignificant, and have yet to

discover their hidden powers

Chapter One

AN UNEXPECTED PRESENT

Berlin, 1941

There was a huge surprise in store for David when his father arrived home on that warm spring day. He was carrying something big covered in a cloth. Placing it on the table in David's bedroom, he whipped the cloth away with a flourish to reveal a cage containing two small white creatures with pink noses and ears.

Never before had David seen real live mice.

'These are your new pets,' said Dr Baum, 'and you must look after them. They will depend on you.'

David was grinning broadly. The mice were his very first pets. The Baum family had never kept a dog or cat because they lived in an apartment in the middle of a big city, Berlin, the capital of Germany. But mice! Sweet and unassuming little animals, happy inside their own cage-home. They could live anywhere. 'Can I hold them, Papa?'

'Yes, but gently.' The doctor smiled at his son, a tender-hearted boy who had his father's wavy dark hair and his mother's hazel eyes.

David opened the cage door and carefully lifted out one of the nervous, quivering mice. It fitted neatly in his hands, but it seemed so vulnerable, so fragile. He returned it to its cage and picked up the other one.

'Are they boy mice or girl mice, Papa?'

'Hmm. Well, I'm not sure. I'm afraid I forgot to ask. It was all such a rush.'

Dr Baum told his son what had happened on his way home. He explained that while hurrying down the street he had bumped into an old acquaintance, and they stopped to exchange news. The man was a scientist who worked in a medical research laboratory, but the lab was being shut down by the authorities. It had been using mice to test out new medicines but now they were surplus to requirements and had to be disposed of somehow.

'You have a young son, don't you?' Dr Baum's acquaintance had asked. 'Would he like a couple of laboratory mice? They make affectionate pets. And they'd be healthy young ones, not yet used in any experiments.'

David's father hesitated for a moment, then nodded. 'I'm sure he would like that. It's kind of you to think of him.' He accompanied the scientist to the medical centre, and waited outside while his friend entered the large stately building. Dr Baum knew it wasn't wise for him to hang about on the pavement, not with so many menacing figures on patrol throughout the city. He glanced around uneasily, alert to any potential danger. But a few minutes later the scientist emerged with the covered cage. 'Just put some newspaper in there for bedding,' he instructed.

Dr Baum thanked him and hurried off. On his way back to the apartment he spotted an abandoned copy of the weekly newspaper *Das Reich* (The Realm) lying on a bench. The paper was the brainchild of the Propaganda Minister, and as Dr Baum had often remarked to his wife and son, was filled with garbage and lies. But it would do just fine as bedding for mice.

Germany had now been at war for almost two years, but even before it began, the Baums' situation had become increasingly troubling. They were Jewish, and Germany was ruled by a dictator who had declared Jews to be the nation's enemies and responsible for all its troubles. According to Adolf Hitler's warped view of the world, Jews weren't real Germans at all, but outsiders who had gained too much control over the country and had to be stopped. So, he had set about getting rid of them. And not just in Germany, but in every country he had conquered during the war he had unleashed on the world.

David had seen Adolf's picture in the newspaper and on posters around the city. He thought his tiny and very silly moustache looked ridiculous.

4

And when he heard him on the radio, he wondered why the dictator always shouted so much.

To carry out his dirty work, Adolf had created legions of brutal henchmen who all belonged to his political organisation, the Nazi Party. These included the stormtroopers, violent thugs known as the Brownshirts; the SS paramilitary fanatics in their black uniforms with the lightning flash insignia on their collars; the Hitler Youth, teenage bullyboys in shorts who loved to start fights and threaten people. But perhaps most dangerous of all were the secret police known as the Gestapo. Its officers tried to blend in with the civilian population and didn't have a particular uniform. But because they usually wore long black leather coats and trilby hats and had a shifty look about them, they weren't too hard to spot.

There was no other political party besides the Nazis – Adolf had banned them all – so there was no one to oppose the dictator and his army of underlings and servile followers. Those who disagreed with the way the country was run were afraid and kept quiet.

In Adolf's evil empire, Jews were no longer allowed to work or own businesses, so they struggled to survive. Dr Baum had been a highly respected family physician whose patients – Jews and non-Jews – trusted and admired him. He had made a good living and provided a comfortable, spacious home for his family, close to the famous park in the centre of Berlin, the Tiergarten. The name means 'animal garden' – centuries ago it was a hunting ground for deer and other wild animals – and the name is still fitting as it is home to the city's zoo. When he was small, David's mother sometimes took him there on sunny days. But the zoo was now off-limits to Jews, as were the cinemas and museums, libraries and cafes, playgrounds and swimming pools, and almost everything else. There was so little for David to do, which was why Dr Baum hoped the pet mice would provide a new interest for his ten-year-old son, and some much-needed entertainment.

Like most young children, David was intrigued by animals. But he didn't know much about mice. Luckily, his father's library in his study at home contained encyclopaedias and all kinds of reference books. David knew that somewhere in all that wealth of knowledge he would find what he needed.

But first of all, he felt he should give names to his two new friends. What should he call them? He'd barely thought about it for a moment before the answer came to him. He would name them after his twin cousins, Benjamin and Robert. Only a year older than him, they had been his closest companions and he missed them terribly. The year before the war broke out their family had managed to leave Berlin for the North of England, where their father, David's Uncle Noah, had been offered work. An engineer with contacts at a civil engineering firm in Lancashire, he'd been lucky to get his family away from the horrors of Adolf's Germany.

'You must get away too, Josef,' Noah had urged his brother, 'before it's too late.' But it wasn't easy to flee to safety. There was a lot of complicated paperwork involved. The necessary documents were difficult, and for many people impossible, to acquire. And Dr Baum had no useful associates abroad who might help him. There were still many Jewish people in Germany – eighty thousand in Berlin alone – and most were desperate to get away. But few countries were willing to take them. Then in 1939 the war came, borders were closed and doors firmly shut to would-be refugees. David's family was trapped.

But one matter, at least, was settled. His two mice would be honoured with the names of his cherished cousins. He would call them Benny and Bobby. It's true, he couldn't tell the mice apart. How could he? They looked the same. But as identical twins, it hadn't always been easy to tell his cousins apart either. So, the names made perfect sense to David.

At first, David's mother, Hannah, didn't think it was such a good idea for her husband to bring the mice home. She had an instinctive aversion to small furry animals, whether in cages or scampering around outside. To Hannah, a rodent was just a rodent. And she certainly couldn't bring herself to touch the creatures. So when David picked them up and held them in his hands, she couldn't stop herself from shuddering with distaste. But then she saw how delighted her son was with the white mice.

David sensed his mother's disapproval and quickly pleaded his case. 'I can keep them, can't I, Mutti? I'll do everything for them myself. They won't trouble you at all!'

Hannah softened. She shrugged and gave David a nod. In the disturbing and dangerous times they were living through she would not be the cause of any further unhappiness for her son. Let him enjoy his new pets. They would take his mind off the war and all their worries.

'Just keep them inside their cage, David,' she said. 'We wouldn't want them to run around and get lost in the apartment, would we?' She looked at her husband, who was standing in the doorway, and he glanced back with a grateful smile.

The next day at school David told his classmates all about Benny and Bobby. 'And they're very friendly!' he declared.

'How do you know they're friendly?' asked one of his classmates, a boy called Bertie.

David thought for a moment. 'Well, they don't bite me, even though they could. They have sharp teeth, you know.' After a pause, he added: 'They let me play with them. Last night, after lights-out, I sneaked them out of their cage and they seemed happy to get to know me better.'

'They're probably terrified of you,' said Bertie, laughing. 'You're like a scary giant to them.'

'Maybe. But they'll soon see they don't need to be afraid of me.'

School was an island of security, one of the few places outside his home where David felt safe. It was a small school and they were taught by Jewish teachers. Jewish children were no longer allowed to attend ordinary schools or mix with other German children. Likewise, no Jewish teacher was allowed to work in a non-Jewish school. This system created by the Nazis seemed normal to David now, because youngsters quickly get used to the circumstances of their lives, even very tough ones. Anyway, he liked his teachers, who were kind and reassuring, though David could sense that they were anxious. In fact, the whole school seemed touched by fear and sadness.

When he told his class teacher, Herr Kleinmann, about Benny and Bobby, the soft-spoken, bespectacled man seemed pleased. 'You must learn all you can about the life of mice,' he advised David. 'Then come and tell the class about them.'

David nodded eagerly. How wonderful! A project all his own.

Chapter Two

DISCOVERING THE MYSTERIES OF MICE

In the evening after supper David opened various
volumes from his father's shelves, looking for anything
interesting he could learn about the common mouse, or
Mus musculus, to give the species its formal Latin
name. He leafed through books on zoology and wildlife
biology, jotting down his findings in a notebook.

The first thing he discovered was that mice were
a lot smarter than people realised. They had a
remarkable sense of smell, which helped them to avoid
danger. For instance, if they smelled a cat, their natural
enemy, they knew to stay well away. And their tiny
sensitive noses could pick up and differentiate even the
faintest odours. Naturally, they could sniff out hidden

sources of food (they loved to eat almost anything). Their hearing was equally acute, and like dogs, they could hear high-frequency sounds that were inaudible to humans. You wouldn't always hear a mouse, but it would always hear you. What's more, they were quick to scarper at the first sign of peril. Excellent climbers, they were able to run up a vertical surface, and could squeeze their bodies through the tiniest of spaces by measuring it with their head.

Their eyesight wasn't very good, but their hypersensitive and constantly twitching whiskers made up for this by vibrating with the air currents and sending crucial information to their nervous system. The vibrations told them what they needed to know about the size and shape of any object, without the need to see or touch it. These highly developed whiskers helped keep them safe. Perhaps they were the reason that mice had survived on earth for 54 million years…not as long as sharks (450 million years) but still a very long time.

David was amazed to discover how mice communicated with each other. They had a language that was partly vocal, in the form of squeaks, chirps, little songs and ultrasonic sounds, but also consisted of scent trails left for each other in their pee. Remarkably, the chemicals in their pee, called pheromones, enabled them to tell other mice who they were, mark out their territories, find breeding mates, and even warn their fellow mice about places to avoid because of lurking danger. Chemical conversations! So far, so fascinating. But David was somewhat put off by the next bit he read: mice had no control over their bladders, so they peed wherever they went. Well, he'd better watch out for that. No wonder his mother told him not to let them run around outside their cage.

Mice had extraordinary memories too. They remembered their own family members among big mice colonies and formed lifelong bonds with them. And they could memorise intricate routes through buildings: beneath floorboards and behind walls, into and out of cracks and cavities, they devised labyrinthine pathways in order to move around unseen. Thoroughly impressed, David acquired a whole new respect for *Mus musculus* and could hardly wait to tell his classmates about the wonders of Benny and Bobby.

But first he would have to feed them. It was dinnertime, and he now knew that their favourite foods included rice and bread, carrots and cabbage, beans, parsley, nuts and apples. But it was wartime and rationing had been introduced, which was bad for everyone but worst of all for the Jews. Not only was their daily food ration far smaller than that allotted to 'pure' Germans (or Aryans, as they were called), but their opportunities for buying provisions had become severely limited as most shops no longer served them. David went to the larder to see what he could find.

He collected a variety of morsels on a saucer, refilled the small water bowl and placed them in the cage. Then he lay down on his bed, chin propped in his hands, and watched Benny and Bobby as they approached the offering slowly and timidly. But they must have been hungry, because soon they were heartily scoffing their meal. He'd only had them for a day but already he was full of affection for his endearing pair of *Mus musculus*. One day, after the war, when he could see his cousins again, he would tell them all about their little namesakes. And they would laugh and joke together and share their stories, and life would be good once more.

Over the coming weeks, David would hurry home from school to see Benny and Bobby and spend some time 'training' them. This entailed getting the mice accustomed to his voice, and especially his scent. He had read in his father's encyclopaedia that a mouse could recognise a human through their unique smell, and once it had learned to trust the identifying scent, it could form a real bond with them.

David would put titbits of food in his hand and reach inside the cage. Then he'd wait for Benny or Bobby (and sometimes both at once) to cautiously approach his hand. After a while, they would put one tiny foot on his palm and sniff the food, leaving the other three feet on the floor, in case a quick getaway was necessary. All the while David spoke to them with quiet reassurance, and before long one of the mice would claim a morsel and scurry off to a corner to eat it. Eventually, they felt comfortable enough to put two feet on David's outstretched hand and remain there, munching away at their treats.

He learned that mice love to burrow and climb and tunnel, so he transformed the cage into a more stimulating home. Using pieces of cardboard, some string, a pair of his old socks, and sticks collected from the nearby Tiergarten park, he built a climbing frame, ladder, tunnel and swing for Benny and Bobby. He created a wonderful playground for them and would happily watch for ages as they amused themselves, even when he should have been doing his schoolwork.

One evening, after the family had eaten a modest supper of potatoes, cabbage and carrots, and his parents had settled in the drawing-room to discuss news of the war in low, apprehensive tones, David suddenly dashed into the room. He was holding the magnifying glass he'd found in his father's antique secretaire desk.

'Papa! Mutti! You'll never guess what I've just discovered!' He looked at his parents in turn. After a dramatic pause, he announced: 'Benny and Bobby are girls!'

Dr Baum gave a faint chuckle and his wife sighed. David told them that, while carrying out further research into the life of the *Mus musculus* in one of the more obscure reference books, he'd discovered how to tell male and female mice apart. It involved an examination of their underside, and although it was tricky it wasn't impossible once you knew what you were looking for – and the magnifying glass had proved useful.

'You will make a fine scientist one day, David,' declared Dr Baum. 'I'm very proud of you.'

It was the last day of the summer term at school and David had been planning for it for weeks. He had promised Herr Kleinmann that he'd give a short talk on 'the life of the mouse' and had closely studied all the notes he'd been taking for this special presentation.

He had learned to be very cautious on his twenty-minute walk through the streets of Berlin to get to his school. Often there were groups of *Jungvolk* boys (the word meant 'young people'), hanging around near the school, waiting to catch hold of a Jewish child to bully and torment. The *Jungvolk*, in their Scout-like uniforms and military caps, were aged ten to fourteen and gearing up for membership of the senior branch of Adolf's youth movement, the Hitler Youth.

This morning, as David was carrying his mice, it was particularly vital to avoid them. So he slipped warily in and out of doorways and hurried along the pavement, walking alongside a preoccupied man with a briefcase on his way to work or a pair of housewives out shopping. He felt safer that way.

He was relieved to bolt through the school doors just as a couple of menacing older boys came strutting around the corner.

A few hours later, after their final lessons for the year, Herr Kleinmann announced that David Baum would be addressing the class on a most intriguing subject. David got up from the back of the classroom, where he'd been sitting quietly all morning, and made his way to the front. He launched enthusiastically into his well-rehearsed talk, and was pleased to see his classmates listening with great attention. None of them had ever thought much about mice before, or the peculiarities of their species. They laughed when David said he'd named Benny and Bobby after his two boy cousins, only to learn that the critters were girls.

'And now,' he concluded, 'I would like to introduce them.' With that, he reached into his jacket pocket and gingerly pulled out a sock. Inside it was a sleeping mouse.

'A-ha!' declared Herr Kleinmann, clapping his hands with amusement. The children burst into squeals of delight, and of course Benny (or maybe it was Bobby) instantly woke up.

'Please take her, sir,' said David, handing the mouse to his beaming teacher. Then David pulled out the second mouse, also sock-bound, from his other pocket. The classroom erupted in cheers, before crowding around to get a better look. A few of the boys asked to hold the mice, but David knew that too many handlers and their strange new scents would frighten the animals – whom he now referred to as B and B – so a minute later they were back inside their socks and in his pockets. (The socks had become slightly damp, but

David decided to ignore the telltale sign of mouse pee for the time being. An indelicate subject and not for the classroom.)

Herr Kleinmann put a hand on his pupil's shoulder. 'Thank you for your illuminating discourse on the life of the mouse,' he said. 'I'm sure we will all now regard them in a new light, and with greater respect.'

David felt elated and proud as he walked home, his usual fears banished. What a brilliant day it had been! Undoubtedly, it was his best day ever at school. What he didn't know was how few school days he had left.

The summer was now truly underway. As he walked past the park, David savoured its rich shades of green and the colourful flowers in bloom – but only from the outside, as he was not allowed in. How he missed the woods and ponds, the playground and the zoo, of which he had only a distant memory. Most of his time was now spent indoors, at the family apartment or occasionally the home of a friend, as public spaces were too dangerous for a Jewish boy. He knew he could

21

only watch the summer go by through the windows of his apartment.

His eleventh birthday arrived and his parents tried to make it cheerful for him. There was a small cake and a present of an attractive, illustrated book: Robert Louis Stevenson's *Treasure Island*, in German. David was delighted, and only a little later understood that it must have been hard for his parents to find the money for it.

Chapter Three

AN ALARMING TURN OF EVENTS

At the start of September came the cruellest blow so far. A decree was passed ordering all Jews over the age of six to wear a six-pointed star made of yellow cloth on their outer clothing whenever they were in public, so that they would be instantly identified as Jewish. This star was the symbol of their religion, Judaism.

Although David could see that his parents were horrified by this new development, and it certainly added an even greater level of fear to their daily lives, he secretly found it a bit flattering. This cherished symbol of the Jewish people was known as the Star of David. It was named after the boy who, in the Judea of Biblical times, slew the giant Goliath with a slingshot and later became King David. Not a man to be trifled with. David Baum hadn't really thought about it before, but now he couldn't help but be pleased that they shared a name. The symbol that Mutti mournfully sewed on to the front of his jacket was the Star of David in more ways than one. He would wear it with pride.

But his defiant mood didn't last long. A few weeks later the Baums, along with the rest of the Jewish population throughout Germany, would discover that Adolf had far worse in store for them than the wearing of the yellow star. The authorities began to round them up, load them on to trains and send them east. They were told they were being 'resettled', but what did that mean?

Late one night, after David went to bed but was unable to sleep, he crept out of his room and listened at the door to the kitchen, where his parents were talking quietly.

'The Nazis claim our people are being taken to labour camps to work for the Reich,' Dr Baum was saying.

'But then why take the children and elderly too?' his wife asked.

'I don't know.' After a while he continued: 'This morning at the Jewish community office I heard someone say they're putting the Jews into ghettos, mostly in Poland, I think. Overcrowded, unsanitary ghettos.'

David felt distraught as his mother begin to weep. 'What shall we do?' she murmured between sobs.

'Hannah, my dear, don't cry. We will think of something. I won't let them send you and David away.'

The words were a comfort to David. He had no idea what his father would – or could – do to save them from the frightening fate of their fellow Jews, but he was relieved to hear him sounding positive and confident. And so he tiptoed back to bed. Before he fell asleep, he peered into B and B's cage and smiled to himself. As nocturnal animals, they were wide awake and zipping about, chasing each other in and out of their cardboard tunnel.

Daily survival had become ever more challenging for the Baum family. There was a time when Dr Baum had more patients than he could easily fit in. But it had been years since Jewish doctors were permitted to treat Aryans, and Berlin had a steadily diminishing population of Jews – every week or so another train left the city carrying a thousand Jewish men, women and children who had been wrenched from their homes. With so few patients left, the doctor was barely able to earn enough to feed his family. They had gradually used up their savings and sold their more valuable possessions.

For a while Dr Baum was given work tutoring the two sons of a sympathetic Aryan neighbour, as the teenagers had been struggling with their science schoolwork. But this was strictly prohibited under Nazi law. They were members of the Hitler Youth, and Adolf's decrees had been strictly drummed into the boys. For the time being they were desperate enough for the help to disregard the fact that their tutor was a Jew. But this could change at any moment, and if the boys gave the game away their father and Dr Baum would pay a heavy price. After a few weeks, the neighbour regretfully put an end to it.

Later that month David's father returned home with a bloodied face and swollen lip. He had been to the Jewish community office, hoping to find a possible escape route out of Germany, but was informed that escape was now hopeless. On the walk back to the apartment, deep in thought, he failed to step off the pavement and into the gutter to make way for an approaching SS officer. The rule was that anyone wearing the yellow star had to give way to the uniformed henchmen – the elites. Dr Baum was struck across the face with a riding crop and knocked to the ground. The officer hit him again with force before he could get back to his feet.

That evening he had no appetite. His dinner untouched, he sat at the kitchen table with his head in his hands, his heart filled with despair. David had never seen his father look so defeated, and it scared him.

But it wasn't long before their fortunes would change.

Chapter Four

A VERY LUCKY ENCOUNTER

At the end of 1941, after the Japanese bombing of the Pearl Harbor naval base in Hawaii, America entered the war. The hounded Jewish population of Berlin, and the rest of Nazi-occupied Europe, was suddenly filled with a new spirit of optimism. Surely, with the mighty Americans joining their side of the fight, the war would soon be won and Adolf's evil empire vanquished.

But Dr Baum remained cautious. 'The Nazis still seem very much in control,' he told his wife, 'particularly here in the Reich. The war could still go on awhile, the danger is by no means over.' And he continued to rack his brains, desperately trying to think of a way to protect his family and prevent them from being deported to a labour camp, or worse.

He called on as many Aryan friends and acquaintances as he could, to ask for help. In particular he visited his former patients, whose illnesses he had cured, whose sick children he had healed, whose wives he had brought back to health after childbirth. He had saved many lives as a young Berlin doctor, and back then no one cared that he was Jewish. But now, when their highly regarded former doctor rang their doorbells, most of them closed the door in his face. Others smiled awkwardly, before mumbling an excuse and disappearing back inside.

One wintry afternoon in the new year, Dr Baum was making his way through the city centre in his threadbare overcoat and hat, a woollen scarf wrapped around his neck. As he passed an elegant cafe where, in happier days, he had often sat with friends, drinking steaming cups of coffee and eating cakes and strudels topped with whipped cream – all a remote fantasy now – his gaze turned towards the window. He paused a moment and looked inside, glimpsing tables full of well-dressed men and women enjoying themselves in the warmth. How strange, he thought to himself, that there were still Berliners living the good life, somehow insulated from the terrors that surrounded him and his family. Then, digging his hands deeper into his pockets, he shivered and walked on.

But from a seat on the other side of the cafe window he had been observed by someone who knew him well, and recognised him despite his now diminished and aged appearance. The man bid a quick goodbye to his table companion, grabbed his hat and coat and made for the door.

'Josef!' he called out as he ran along the pavement after the doctor's retreating back. 'Josef, wait!'

At first Dr Baum thought he had imagined it. But no, somebody really was calling his name. As he turned round, the man caught up with him and grabbed hold of his shoulders. 'My dear good friend, how happy I am to see you again,' he said in a tone so genuine and friendly that Dr Baum's eyes filled with tears.

He gazed at this smiling man from his past. 'Emil?' he whispered.

The two men embraced. Then Emil checked himself and pulled away. It was dangerous to be seen in public fraternising with a man wearing the yellow star, much less embracing him.

'And your wife, Hannah – how is she?'

'We still survive, Emil, with our boy, David.'

'Josef, I'm going to give you an address. Do not write it down. Memorise it. Meet me there tomorrow afternoon at four o'clock, and make sure no one sees you enter the building. You and your family are in the gravest danger. But I'm going to help you.' He whispered an address a half-hour's walk from the Baums' apartment. 'Till tomorrow,' he said. Then he turned and walked swiftly away.

For the first time in as long as he could remember, Josef Baum felt his spirits soar. With a quickened tempo he headed for home, no longer feeling the cold. He couldn't wait to tell Hannah what had happened.

She was in the kitchen, peeling potatoes for that evening's soup, when Dr Baum burst in with his news. 'My dear, do you remember my old friend from medical school, Emil Vogel? We were best pals for years, then he went to work at a hospital in Cologne and we lost touch. Well, he's back in Berlin now and I met him on the street, and I have no idea how or what or anything, but he is going to help us!'

Hannah put down the potato and gave her husband a baffled look. 'Emil? Oh yes, I remember him. A tall, nice-looking young man with blond hair.' She shrugged. 'But what can he do for us, your doctor friend?'

'We'll find out soon – I'm meeting him again tomorrow. No doubt he'll tell me then.' And to her surprise, her husband laughed out loud for the first time in a long while. 'By the way, Emil is no longer the young man you remember. He is just as old as me.'

At precisely four o'clock the next day Josef Baum, his hat pulled low over his forehead, approached the entrance to the building at the address Emil had given him. It was a quiet side street and there were very few people around. He found himself in an inner courtyard, with apartment blocks on all sides. It was a typical Berlin residential complex. He found the block and the buzzer he was looking for.

'Hello?' he heard a woman's voice say.

'Hello. My name is Baum.'

'First floor, then turn left.'

Dr Baum pushed open the door, stepped into a dimly lit hallway and hurried up a curved staircase. A moment later he was standing, hat in hand, in the vestibule of a tidy, bright apartment.

A middle-aged woman with greying hair approached him and held out her hand. 'Welcome, Josef. My name is Anna. Come inside and meet the others.'

Dr Baum nodded. 'Thank you.'

In the book-filled drawing-room, seated around a ceramic-tiled stove where a comforting coal fire was burning, were three men. Emil Vogel was one of them, and he jumped to his feet and hugged his old friend.

Then he introduced the two younger men, Gunther and Peter. 'Of course, these are not their real names. It's safer for us to use aliases. But they are friends, which is all you need to know.'

Over cups of hot tea and slices of marble cake, Dr Baum learned that Emil and the others belonged to the Resistance, secret cells of anti-Nazis operating against Adolf's regime. Some of these resisters printed underground leaflets exposing the government's lies, some sabotaged military installations and others carried out spying missions for the British and Americans. Crucially, some were expert forgers able to produce the vital identity documents that could save Adolf's endangered enemies: political opponents, fugitives, rebels, Jews.

With a smile, Emil placed a hand firmly on Josef's arm and reassured him: 'You see, there are still some good Germans here in the Reich.'

The man called Gunther put down his teacup and leaned closer to Josef. 'Listen, my friend,' he began in an urgent tone. 'Since last year more and more Jews have been deported from Berlin to ghettos in other cities. That was terrible enough. But now they are being taken straight to concentration camps, where they are so ill-treated they're not expected to last long. If you want your family to survive, until this war is over and Adolf Hitler is defeated you must cease being Jews and acquire Aryan identities. As you know, it's virtually impossible to leave Germany. But with your new names, you can move to another part of it where they don't know you. And I'm afraid that you, your wife and son will have to split up, as it's safer that way. Do you understand?'

Dr Baum nodded slowly, trying to take it all in.

After a moment Emil spoke. 'Josef, I'm a member of the Nazi Party,' he admitted matter-of-factly. 'Almost all German doctors are now, it's the only way to forge ahead in the profession. But I am no Nazi at heart. I've despised this government ever since they put my father in one of their monstrous camps back in 1936, for publicly criticising their policies. He was imprisoned in that hell for eighteen months. Starved, beaten, humiliated. It broke him and he died two years later. That was when I knew I had to join the

Resistance. But my Party membership has been good cover, shielding me from suspicion, which makes it easier for me to fight for our cause.'

The third cell member, Peter, was introduced as their forger. 'I'm a graphic designer,' he explained. 'Before the war, I designed adverts for magazines, theatre billboards and fancy brochures for business owners. But the Nazis are in charge everywhere now and I won't work for people I hate. So I scrape by, doing odd jobs. But I still have my design skills and excellent eyesight. The Resistance provides me with the equipment I need – paper, ink, official stamps – and a secret workshop in the city. I can forge identity cards, travel permits, ration cards, birth certificates – all convincing enough to get someone past a checkpoint. I can turn a Jew into an Aryan with a few hours' work.' He smiled at Josef and added: 'I will help the Baum family disappear. But we must act quickly, before the Gestapo knocks on your door.'

Dr Baum was instructed to return to Anna's apartment the following day with two passport-sized photos, one of himself and one of Hannah. David didn't need one because an Aryan under eighteen (as per his new identity) wasn't required to carry photo identification. Peter promised to have their new identity documents finished two days later, and that a trusted courier would deliver them to the Baum apartment the same evening. By then the family must be ready to leave, carrying only one small suitcase each.

At the door, as the doctor was leaving, Emil clasped his friend's hands. 'I'm so glad you passed by the cafe window, Josef. Take courage. We'll get through this!'

Chapter Five

ESCAPE INTO THE NIGHT

Josef Baum did not doubt that the plan set out by Emil and his friends in the Resistance was his family's best chance. Almost every day he heard of friends, neighbours or patients who had been rounded up and carted off to some sinister destination from which no one ever returned. He would not wait around for that to happen to them. He had convinced Hannah that their only hope lay with Emil and his comrades in the Resistance. 'Putting my child into the hands of strangers,' she sobbed, her head on her husband's shoulder. 'That it has come to this …'

But he thought it best not to tell his son right away about their planned disappearance. It was better for the boy not to worry too much in advance. Naturally, he would fret about being separated from his parents and their uncertain future. And he might accidentally give the secret operation away. So Dr Baum told him only that he must expect a major change in their lives. It was coming soon, and he would have to put his trust in his parents and the courageous friends helping them.

Early on the allotted evening Dr Baum went to his son's room and sat down on his bed. David was standing by his table. 'I've been teaching the mice a new trick for the past few days, Papa,' he announced. 'And they are ready to perform!' Benny and Bobby were playing on the table in front of him. He lifted them up and placed them gently beside each other. The mice studied David intently. He raised his forefingers and made circling motions, while calling out 'Turn!' And the two mice twirled around in a circle like ballerinas, then stopped, at which point David rewarded them with treats of breadcrumbs.

He and his father laughed.

It would be their last laugh together for a long time. Sitting his son down beside him, Dr Baum began to outline the arrangements for their escape from the city, for which he said they should be thankful. They would be leaving behind their present existence in Berlin and everything they had known. But he must be brave and see it as a great adventure.

David had become hardened to adversity and was unafraid of this new 'adventure'. But he did fear one potential consequence. 'Will I be able to take Benny and Bobby with me?'

'No, I'm afraid it's not possible.'

David crumpled and buried his face in his pillow. Suddenly, he was too dejected even to speak.

Later they ate supper, mostly in pensive silence. After clearing up in the kitchen, Hannah and her husband packed their cases with a few bare essentials.

An hour later there was a knock on their door. Dr Baum opened it a crack and saw a young man carrying a briefcase. 'Peter sent me,' he whispered as he stepped inside.

He informed the Baums that anti-Nazi sympathisers had been found to shelter each of them under their new identities. Then he handed them the documents that would save their lives. Tonight the Baum family, as it had been known, would vanish.

The young man opened his case and pulled out Dr and Frau Baum's new identity cards. He was to be Hermann Winkler, former schoolteacher, recently widowed, in poor health and on his way to recuperate with a cousin on the Baltic coast near Rostock. Hannah became Gertrud Albrecht, unmarried, newly appointed housekeeper's assistant for a well-to-do German family in the town of Potsdam, twenty miles southwest of Berlin.

The nameless young man from the Resistance reached into his case again and took out their travel passes, allowing them to board trains leaving the city, along with their train tickets. He also gave them their official food ration coupons, still quite generous for Aryans, despite wartime shortages. Peter had forged everything faultlessly. 'Leave your yellow stars behind,' the courier told the Baums, 'you won't need them anymore. And make your way separately to the train station. Say your goodbyes here.'

As for David, the boy's new identity was that of an orphan called Franz Becker, whose ageing grandparents were no longer able to care for him. They were sending him to live on a distant relative's farm in the deepest countryside, two hundred miles to the southwest, where he would help with farm work and grow healthy and strong. The young Resistance fighter would be escorting him there personally: the people taking David in were the man's own uncle and aunt.

The Baums embraced each other. When would they be together again? How long would the war last? Would they stay safe? No one had any answers.

'Don't cry, Mutti, I'll be all right,' said David, but he was fighting back tears himself.

Dr Baum stroked his son's hair and spoke softly. 'Have faith, dear child. Your mother and I will be thinking of you every day, until we're back together again.'

'I know, Papa.'

And so they bade farewell to the home and the life they knew, and stepped out into the dark night of the unknown. The last thing David did before he left the apartment was lift Benny and Bobby out of their cage and for a moment hold them tenderly to his cheeks. 'Goodbye, my friends. Forgive me for leaving you. But you *Mus musculus* are very clever, you are true survivors. I know you will look after yourselves.' He put them back inside their cage and gave them a final melancholy look before leaving his room, and his home.

He left their cage door open.

Chapter Six

A FIENDISH FAMILY MOVES IN

One Sunday in the spring of 1942, a few weeks after the Baums' departure, the front door of their apartment was flung open and a tall solidly built man marched in. 'Take a look around, my liebling. It's wonderful, isn't it?' He waved his arm in triumph. 'Wait till you see the size of the drawing-room.'

Behind him strode a woman with well-coiffed blonde hair, wearing a smart tailored outfit. She glanced around and pursed her lips, careful not to smudge her lipstick. 'Rather old-fashioned but I suppose we can make it work.'

The last to saunter in was a sandy-haired boy of fifteen. He didn't say anything but gave the place a cursory glance before reaching into his pocket and taking out a rolled-up copy of *Will and Power*, the monthly magazine of the Hitler Youth. Then he sat in a comfy armchair, kicked off his shoes and started reading.

The Streicher family were among the happy beneficiaries of the thousands of newly emptied flats and houses that had been occupied by Jews before they were forced to flee or were rounded up and deported. As an officer of the Gestapo, Kurt Streicher was in a good position to grab one of them for himself. There were definite perks to the job. Years ago, he'd been an ordinary municipal policeman, but Officer Streicher was nothing if not ambitious. He saw how he could rise in the Nazi pecking order and become more prominent and powerful as a member of the fearsome secret police. And now here he was, moving his family into a much nicer apartment in a much better part of town.

His wife, Frida, however, was not easy to please. Some of the properties hastily left behind by Jews still had fine paintings on the walls, valuable silverware and superior porcelain collections. But the doctor who'd lived here, Streicher noted disdainfully, seemed to have sold off what valuables he had. A big disappointment for Frida, who loved pretty things, the more expensive the better. Still, he was earning good money now and could afford a few luxuries. Better still, he could confiscate them from elsewhere and enjoy them himself. *Long live the Nazi good life!* he often chortled to himself.

He knew his son, Rolf, would be pleased with their new residence, as he'd have a bigger bedroom, which meant more space for his Hitler Youth paraphernalia. That stuff seemed to accumulate by the day – the Swastika-adorned tent and the rest of his camping equipment, his military-style knapsack, varied sports items, uniforms, banners and badges, his bugle (to be played while marching) and drum (likewise, when not blowing the bugle), the special dagger he was so proud of, engraved with the words *Blut und Ehre!* (blood and honour), and his growing collection of Nazi-approved magazines and books. Rolf was a big reader. When asked to name his favourite book, he would boldly state that it was Adolf's bestselling work,

entitled *Mein Kampf*, which meant 'My Struggle'…
although he wouldn't admit that he found the Nazi
leader's writing rather hard to follow.

After a while Rolf got up and went to inspect
his own quarters. A moment later he protested to his
parents: 'There's some sort of cage in my room. I don't
know what useless animal was living in it, but can you
please get rid of it immediately? It's disgusting.'

Over the following days the new residents remade the
apartment in their own image. They installed additional
pieces of furniture – as well as Kurt Streicher's brand-
new Blaupunkt radio, so as not to miss any of the
broadcasts ordered by the Propaganda Minister. The
large framed photograph of Adolf, looking stern and
invincible, was given pride of place above the sofa in
the drawing-room. Frida, a prominent member of the
Nazi Women's League, placed hand-embroidered
cushions celebrating German motherhood around the
apartment. (She didn't embroider them herself – she
found that needlework sometimes resulted in broken
fingernails – but was gifted them from fellow League

members. These ladies valued good relations with the wife of a man who worked for a secret government department, although Frida was evasive about what exactly Kurt did.) For his part, Rolf turned his bedroom into a mini Hitler Youth command centre and had a full-length mirror brought in, all the better to inspect his appearance before venturing forth in uniform.

Another major transformation was the lavishly supplied larder. Its shelves and cupboards, once so sparsely stocked, were now bursting with spicy sausages, frankfurters and salamis, French cheeses, butter and lard, tins of Danish ham, sardines and herrings, white beans and lentils, oatmeal and sugar, jars of jam and honey, mounds of potatoes, turnips and cabbages and other assorted produce from Berlin's market halls.

Not surprisingly, it wasn't long before this cornucopia was detected by two 'useless animals' called Benny and Bobby.

B and B had been having a challenging time since their companion and roommate's departure. At first, they had no idea what had happened. Why did he disappear? Where did he go? Why wasn't he bringing them their daily food and water and playing with them and teaching them fun new tricks? It was all so distressing. No sounds, no familiar scents, nothing. They felt very alone as they spent a whole day cuddled together, sleeping uneasily, waiting. But when night fell their survival instincts kicked in and they roused themselves to action. They noticed that their cage door was open, and having run out of food (and because mice are always hungry) they decided they had better scout around for some eats.

They scurried into the various rooms, inspecting each one from corner to corner, their long sensitive whiskers twitching, picking up faint messages carried in the air. They quickly found what little food was left in the kitchen, but that didn't last long. Then they got truly adventurous. They came across a tiny gap between the wall and the parquet floor in the drawing-room, and squeezing themselves through, encountered a whole universe they never knew existed. Tunnels bigger and deeper and darker and far more thrilling than the miniature cardboard one they darted through in their cage. There were passageways and climbing frames to explore, which seemed to reach into infinity. Mysterious exits and entrances too enticing to resist. They felt that maybe their new life would work out after all.

Best of all, it wasn't long before they made new friends. But not human ones, like David. This time they were of the *Mus musculus* kind. It's true, they looked different – not pink-eyed and white-furred, like laboratory mice such as them, but dark-eyed and with fur of light brown – the colour, indeed, known as 'mousy'. But they were comrades all the same, so B and B weren't lonely anymore. And with a bit of coaching from these new housemates, they learned to fend for themselves, sneaking late at night into adjoining apartments in the old five-storey building near the Tiergarten, using their sensory powers to sniff out tasty edibles and locate dripping taps and leaky pipes for water.

They worked out the most rewarding routes to scamper along – up and down, through the labyrinthine tunnels, into one crevice and out another. One of these routes led them back to their former habitat on the second floor, to David's bedroom, his table and their cage. They had been happy there, and their memories were sharp, so they never forgot the place. But whenever they returned to it, it was devoid of human life … until one night it wasn't.

On that occasion, when they entered through the gap between the wall and the parquet floor, they could tell instantly that something dramatic had taken place. They picked up an abundance of new scents and sounds – the unmistakable signs of human habitation. From the master bedroom came the combined smells of perfume, face powder and hair lacquer, and the sound of heavy breathing with occasional snores. In David's room the cage was gone, and B and B's delicate whiskers began to quiver fiercely from sensory overload: what were all these strange new objects of all shapes and sizes? They were forced into a hasty retreat. And then inevitably, and most beneficially, they were drawn to the sumptuously stocked kitchen larder. They could barely believe their noses as they tucked into a midnight feast.

Before the misty dawn light fell on the city of Berlin, B and B, their stomachs gloriously full, scarpered back to their hidden nest beyond the walls.

A couple of hours later a bleary-eyed Frau Streicher ambled into the kitchen to make her morning coffee. When she opened the larder door and reached for her packet of coffee – *real* coffee, not the fake stuff which people without important connections were forced to drink – she got a shock and let out a piercing scream. The bags of oatmeal and sugar had been gnawed open and the contents spilled, and the hazelnut biscuits she'd been saving for her forthcoming tea with the ladies of the Nazi Women's League were in pieces – clearly the dirty work of beastly nocturnal creatures.

'Kurt! Come at once!'

A moment later her anxious husband was standing at her side.

'Look!'

Kurt Streicher surveyed the scene, frowned and shook his head. 'These old buildings, liebling, they often have a mouse or two running around. Don't you worry. We'll soon get rid of them.'

'I am not touching anything in there until you do!'

Later that day a forced-labour worker, a Polish woman in her twenties but who looked much older, was brought in to scrub the larder shelves clean and cover the provisions with tablecloths. Afterwards, Officer Streicher set three strategically placed mouse traps. He told himself he'd better deal with the traps early the next day before his wife got up, or else there would be another bloodcurdling scream at the sight of the bodies.

That night, B and B made their way back to the Streichers' lavish food supplies for a refill. Their companions, the house mice, were experienced at avoiding the lethal traps set by human co-inhabitants and had taught B and B how to detect these perils and stay safe. So they cautiously sidestepped the mouse traps, gnawed through the tablecloths and tucked in once more, this time sampling a delicious Hungarian salami with a few crumbs of rye bread. For dessert, they nibbled at a bar of Swiss chocolate. (They ignored the cheeses, which they had little interest in. People always think mice love cheese, which is why it's put in mouse traps. But in fact, rather like children, mice far prefer chocolate.) When at last B and B finished their meal, shortly before dawn, they were so full they could only waddle back to their nest. They slept exceedingly well that day.

Kurt Streicher, like any officer of the dreaded Gestapo, was not used to being ridiculed or defied. He was apoplectic when he saw the state of the larder the next morning. 'Right!' he fumed under his breath. 'Time for a new plan of action.' He knew exactly what to do next. It was time to bring in a ruthless stalking feline. One whiff of cat and no mouse would dare creep into the Streicher apartment again and steal their food. But how to acquire one? He resolved to look into the matter without delay. Meanwhile, he'd better get that Polish woman back to clean the larder again.

Chapter Seven

ENTER THE RUTHLESS FELINE

'It's very generous of you to give her to us.'

'But, Herr Streicher! I am not *giving* her to you. This is purely a temporary arrangement. You may look after Schatzi for the *time being*.' The plump matronly woman installed on the Streichers' sofa was a proud daughter of the von Schlocken family of minor Prussian nobles, now married to an intelligence officer, Werner Hubermeyer. She was lovingly stroking an equally well-fed, fluffy white Persian cat lying on her lap.

'Of course, dear lady. Understood.' Officer Streicher gazed at the sleepy-looking cat. 'What a fine-looking creature your Schatzi is,' he remarked airily, although he took no interest in cats at all. He was more of a dog man, and especially fond of dogs that could track down runaways.

'You appreciate that if not for the ghastly bombs that have started dropping on Berlin, I would not be leaving the city for our country house near Dannenberg. And that if it weren't for those two ferocious Alsatians my husband keeps there, always snarling and barking and who *loathe* cats, I would be taking Schatzi with me.'

'Yes, Frau Hubermeyer, I certainly do appreciate that.'

Schatzi is the German word for 'little treasure', and Frau Hubermeyer had always given her adored cat the VIP treatment, as befitted a pet of the minor Prussian nobility. And she was no ordinary moggy. Persian cats are especially magnificent and have been long favoured by royalty. Schatzi ate only the finest cuts of meat and the best fillets of fish. Her favourite meal consisted of tender slivers of duck, gently sautéed and served with creamed carrots.

'Her silky fur requires frequent brushing. And please remember she has a delicate stomach, Herr Streicher. For breakfast, only morsels of bread soaked in warm milk. And before bedtime a bowl of chicken broth. But never any sausage, please – far too spicy.'

'That is noted.' He paused before moving on to a more crucial matter. 'I believe you said she was a skilled mouser?'

'Oh my goodness, I should say so. I have never forgotten the time a mouse ran across the floor of our dining room, bold as can be, and Schatzi leaped off her chair and gave chase. That mouse disappeared out of the house and never came back, I assure you!'

'Impressive. And when was that?'

Frau Hubermeyer thought for a moment. 'About six years ago.'

Rolf had been dawdling in the doorway, listening. He didn't place much faith in that overstuffed, pampered cat. On the other hand, he liked the sound of Herr Hubermeyer's Alsatians. They were much more his kind of pet.

58

When Frau Streicher arrived home from the hair salon and the dress shop, she instantly spotted Schatzi dozing in the best armchair, on top of a Women's League cushion. 'Kurt!' she shouted. 'Who allowed a strange cat to take over that chair and lie on my cushion?'

Her husband came into the room with a sheepish expression (not a typical look for him). 'Frau Hubermeyer suggested the arrangement, liebling. But don't fret, we'll make another bed for her cat.'

Frau Streicher hoped her husband's latest scheme for getting rid of the wretched mice would succeed. She peered down at Schatzi, whose sky-blue eyes were blinking up at her drowsily, and petted her head. It wasn't out of affection, but rather the knowledge that she needed to have the animal on her side. 'Nice cat,' she mumbled, then went straight to the bathroom to wash her hands.

On B and B's next night-time visit to the apartment, they realised immediately that a feline had taken up residence. The scent was unmistakable. But they'd never had dealings with a cat before. Was it strictly necessary to give up on the rich pickings in the larder? Perhaps they could simply outrun this new intruder, should it make an unwanted appearance at their food stocks.

That night all was quiet as they entered via the usual crevice and scooted along the drawing-room floor to the kitchen. They passed Schatzi, who was sleeping peacefully on her Nazi Women's League cushion (oh yes, it was *hers* now). Her nose twitched as, for the merest moment, she vaguely sensed that some form of prey had entered the vicinity. But then she stretched her front legs, yawned and returned to her slumber. It must have been a dream.

B and B tucked into a bag of roasted peanuts they discovered in a corner of the larder and decided they liked the tasty treats very much. Afterwards, they scurried away without incident. Their confidence increased when they noticed, as they sped past, that the cat was still sleeping and none the wiser.

But a few nights later, Schatzi had her big moment. Overweight, cossetted and lazy she might have been, but deep inside, beneath all that glossy fur, she retained the age-old instincts of a cold-blooded predator. It is something no cat, however spoilt, ever entirely loses.

On the night in question, an unexpected noise woke Schatzi. It was the Nazi banner in Rolf's room, which had been leaning awkwardly against the wall and suddenly toppled over. Next, a low curse came from the same direction. Schatzi's back arched slightly. She did her best to avoid the teenager. He wasn't very pleasant, and once he had even shoved her off her favoured armchair, out of spite. If only Frau Hubermeyer had witnessed the assault. There would have been such trouble!

Schatzi stretched all four limbs and got up. She padded towards the kitchen, wondering whether there was any chicken broth left in her bowl. A lick or two would come in nicely.

All of a sudden, she stopped dead in her tracks. She crouched down and crept forward slowly and silently, head low, eyes sharply focused straight ahead. It was no dream this time. There really was prey afoot. Mice, to be precise. *Oh goody*, she thought. *Let's have some fun*. She was on high alert now, every muscle tensed and ready to spring.

At the same time B and B, on the floor in front of the larder entrance, picked up the overpowering scent of cat and their whiskers quivered alarmingly. Turning round, they confronted the huge beast watching them and froze with terror. There was no escape, neither to the left nor to the right. The cat was blocking their path, and creeping closer …

Trying desperately to keep their nerve, with their last ounce of daring B and B signalled to each other that they would make a dash for freedom. One of them, at least, must survive this mortal encounter. Benny would run to the left, Bobby to the right. It was a deadly game of chance and there wasn't a second to waste. In a flash, they shot forwards.

But Schatzi was just as quick. She leaped to her feet, and as Bobby sped past, she slammed a fat paw on Benny. The mouse let out a distressed and doom-laden squeak as she lay captured beneath it.

Schatzi was very pleased with herself and felt positively invigorated. She recalled the happy days of her youth, when she'd caught birds in the Hubermeyers' garden and brought them inside as offerings for her mistress. And there was the unforgettable occasion when she'd chased that frightened mouse out of the dining room. How fondly the Hubermeyers had stroked and praised her ... she almost purred at the memories.

She half raised her paw briefly to look at Benny, then put it firmly back down. She had no intention of snacking on the mouse. Heavens, no. After duck and beef, chicken and sardines, the taste of mouse was scarcely appealing. However, it made an excellent toy. And when she grew bored playing with it she'd grab it with her sharp pointy teeth, give it a good crunch and present it as a token of her appreciation to the new mistress, who was a decent enough cook and didn't stint on the portions.

Schatzi lifted her paw once more and gave the captive mouse a couple of slaps. Benny trembled and moved an inch to the side. That was all the encouragement the pitiless predator needed. Down came the big paw again. Poor Benny could barely breathe, her heart was beating dangerously fast and she began to feel that the end was near.

Just then Frau Streicher walked into the kitchen, wrapped in her silk dressing gown. She too had been woken up by the falling banner in Rolf's room. Unable to get back to sleep, she fancied a cup of tea.

'Hello, Schatzi,' she murmured. 'What are you doing here? Hungry again, I suppose?'

Frau Streicher busied herself with the kettle, then headed for the larder, where the tea was kept. 'Move away now, Schatzi. You're in my way.' But the cat wouldn't budge. 'Schatzi!' Still no movement, only a low, steady growling from the back of her throat. 'Don't you growl at me. I'm still in charge here.' And with that she scooped up the cat, carried it to the drawing-room and deposited it on the embroidered Women's League cushion (which she no longer wanted because it was covered in cat hair). She never even noticed the miniscule creature she had liberated from under the mighty paw.

A few seconds was all it took for Benny to come to her senses after this traumatic experience. And then she took off, running faster than she had ever run before, panting and peeing all the way. She shot through the gap in the wall and along the familiar route to the cosy habitat she shared with her closest companion, Bobby, who was overjoyed to see her. They curled up together, feeling lucky to be alive. They knew they were far enough away from the Streichers to be safe, yet near enough to go back, should they wish.

It had been a close call for the mice. A most frightening episode. But somehow they sensed their escapades were by no means over.

Chapter Eight

THE TREASURE HUNT

Officer Kurt Streicher of the Gestapo was leaning back
in the leather chair at the antique secretaire desk in
what had formerly been Dr Baum's study. He was truly
impressed by this grand item of furniture with its shiny
walnut veneer. It consisted of two hefty parts, an upper
and a lower. The lower one had a hinged desktop that
opened out to form a workspace. Both parts had vertical
rows of drawers – short and shallow ones at the top and
longer, deeper ones below – and there were small
shelves and cubby holes as well. Streicher had earlier
amused himself by riffling through the contents: dull-
looking medical notes and papers, patients' records
from many years ago, cuttings from scientific journals,
family photos, David Baum's school reports, holiday

trinkets and even – such sentimentality! – a bundle of old love letters from the doctor's wife, Hannah. Naturally, he had chucked out the lot because he needed the space for his own things. A busy secret policeman's work always involved a lot of things, mostly secret ones.

Streicher reckoned the handsome desk was worth a pretty penny. But he wouldn't sell it, not yet anyway. He wanted to impress other people with it – important visitors to his sophisticated new dwelling. People such as his high-up contacts in the Gestapo and the SS, as well as the SD, the Nazi Party's intelligence service. He planned to host a sumptuous dinner party, inviting his boss and other men of influence working alongside him at the Reich Security Main Office, headquarters of Adolf's many interweaving secret security organisations.

How he loved that massive, imposing building on Prinz-Albrecht Street. It had a formidable reputation, striking fear into the hapless citizens summoned there. He enjoyed nothing more than strutting in each morning, nodding to the armed guards at the entrance, skipping up the broad steps to his office, smiling at the pretty secretaries, and settling down to work on his case files.

He was never short of files on missing suspects and 'persons of interest'. People suspected of involvement in the Resistance, Jews in hiding or using false identities, political opponents, defiant clergymen and other troublemakers – in short, enemies of the state. He would collect information on each one, put together dossiers and then do his best to find and arrest them. He'd had a fair amount of success in this and found it thoroughly satisfying to catch people who tried to flee the Nazi net. He would stalk his suspects, set traps for them, then reel them in. The late-night arrests, the interrogations, the *ta-da!* moment when he presented his superiors with a signed confession. He relished it all. And so that everyone would see how dedicated he was to his job, he often took the files home to work on them further.

One case, in particular, kept niggling at him. Where was the Baum family? The Gestapo had come for them one night, hammering on their door, only to find they had vanished into thin air. He was determined to track them down, along with those who had helped them slip away.

He also wondered whether the Baums had a secret hiding place in the apartment, where they stashed valuables. Jewellery, foreign currency, documents revealing details of bank accounts, share certificates and who knew what else. Of course, they might have emptied it when they fled, but perhaps in their panic to get away they forgot to take everything, or didn't have time. Streicher examined all the rooms from top to bottom, but so far had discovered nothing. No wall safe concealed behind a picture, no camouflaged storage space inside a wardrobe or loose floorboard with a secret cavity underneath. But he wasn't ready to give up yet. Those Jews might be cunning, but they couldn't outsmart him.

His gaze now fell on the shelves lining the walls. Such a lot of books! Who had the time to do so much reading? He'd never been much of a reader himself and groaned at the thought of spending hours examining all these volumes in order to weed out the banned authors. That was why he had instructed Rolf, more than once, to get on and do it, but the boy claimed to be too busy with schoolwork and his Hitler Youth activities. What free time he had was spent taking that pretty blonde girl from school to the cinema or for ice cream sundaes at fashionable cafes. But Rolf would have to get it done soon, because they couldn't possibly give that important dinner party while there were banned books in the apartment, liable to be spotted by his eagle-eyed colleagues. What a disastrous career move that would be – he would find himself under investigation in a flash.

And so, with further urging from his father, after supper that evening Rolf let himself into the study, sighed and settled down to the tedious task at hand. He had a pretty good idea which books had to be hurled ruthlessly into the fire, so to speak. (The famous book burnings of the previous decade, when Adolf-adoring university students had scoured the nation's libraries and consigned thousands of banned books to bonfires, had been discussed by his schoolteachers. It sounded awesome and Rolf wished he could have seen it.) All

Jewish authors were prohibited, naturally. As were all socialists and communists. Any author of a liberal or democratic or anarchist or pacifist inclination was outlawed, as were all works critical of Adolf and his regime.

Rolf began scanning the titles. Many of the books filling Dr Baum's shelves were of a medical nature and he reckoned he needn't bother with them, even though, quite possibly, they contained outdated views. Then he saw a book by Sigmund Freud and guffawed. How predictable! That Jew had invented a crazy pseudoscience called psychoanalysis, some nonsense about analysing the subconscious mind. It had been totally discredited by Nazi medical experts. He plucked it off the shelf with an air of disgust and flung it on the floor. Then he saw a short book by Albert Einstein: *The World as I See It*. Ha! We don't care how you see the world, Dr Einstein, we only care how Adolf sees it. On to the floor it plunked.

Other volumes followed. There was a shelf of novels and Rolf removed all those by American and British writers, because Adolf's Fatherland was at war with those countries and that was reason enough. So out went Ernest Hemingway, Scott Fitzgerald, Aldous Huxley and D.H. Lawrence. Next Rolf pulled out a book by a Russian writer called Leo Tolstoy. He didn't know much about him, but Tolstoy was Russian, and treacherous Russia, as every good German knew, was the biggest foe of all. The rejects on the floor were piling up.

Then his attention was caught by a book with a familiar title. He recalled that a friend in the Hitler Youth had cautiously mentioned it to him and said it was wicked and deceitful and to be avoided at all costs. Called *All Quiet on the Western Front*, it was about the Great War of 1914-1918, and apparently, its German author, Erich Maria Remarque, portrayed the German soldiers as frightened and spineless. As losers! What's more, the book made war itself seem a gruesome thing. How rotten and unpatriotic this Remarque fellow was, thought Rolf.

Like all his mates, he was fiercely proud of the noble war his country was waging to re-establish its greatness and honour. The Hitler Youth was even now preparing him in case he was needed to join the fight later, when he turned eighteen. The very thought of it thrilled him. He dreamed of making his family, his friends and his country proud of him one day.

He held the Remarque book in his hands, turning it over once or twice and fanning through its pages. At the front there was a brief introduction: *This book is intended as an accusation, as well as a confession. It is an attempt to report on a generation that was destroyed by war – even if it escaped its grenades.* What on earth did he mean by that? Rolf wondered, frowning.

He was about to add it to the pile of books on the floor, but at the last moment stopped himself. *Maybe I'll keep this one for now*, he thought. *No harm in it, if nobody knows.*

After another hour or so of fastidious culling, Rolf, at last, left the study and informed his father, who was in the drawing-room listening to a speech on his fancy new radio, that he had finally completed the task he'd been set. He went to his bedroom with *All Quiet on the Western Front* concealed inside his pullover and found a safe spot for it on the shelf at the top of his wardrobe, beneath his collection of Hitler Youth magazines.

It was the middle of the night and in his attic bedroom in the house on the Baltic coast, near the town of Rostock, Dr Josef Baum woke with a start and sat upright. 'Oh no no no!' he moaned. 'How stupid of me!' What jolted him out of his sleep was the realisation that he had left behind something of great importance – and great value – in the apartment in Berlin. Somehow, in the drama of the family's departure, he had forgotten all about it.

Although he had used up their savings and sold off their valuable possessions over the past few years in order to buy food and pay the rent, there was one last precious item he had retained. It was a family heirloom handed down from his grandmother to his mother, a diamond-encrusted necklace worth a lot of money. It wasn't only that he couldn't bring himself to sell it for sentimental reasons. He knew that, should they survive this dreadful war, they would need money to start a new life, maybe in another country. The necklace was the little fortune which could help them do that.

He realised soon after Adolf seized power that he couldn't trust his German bank, so he'd removed the necklace from his safety deposit box and hidden it away in the apartment, in the only place where he thought it would be safe. He knew only too well that the apartment would now be inhabited by strangers. No doubt some lucky Aryans had moved in and made themselves comfortable in his old home. Would he ever again see his treasured heirloom? Or would the unknown interlopers chance across it and rub their hands with glee? He agonised and rebuked himself as he lay in the dark, and found no more sleep that night.

Chapter Nine

A MOST IMPORTANT DINNER IS PLANNED

For a fortnight or so, B and B stayed away from the
Streicher household. The incident with the cat had
certainly rattled them. But the attractions of their larder
were hard to resist, being plainly superior to those of
the two apartments on either side, as well as the ones
immediately above and below (naturally, they had
dropped in on them all, after consulting with the
knowledgeable house mice). So go back to it they knew
they must. But next time they would avoid the room
with the sleeping cat – no point in pushing their luck.
They were sure to find another entry point into the
apartment and a different route to the kitchen.

At last, they decided to go for it. Sniffing and searching and scuttling around, B and B encountered a slight crack in a skirting board that took them beneath the floor to the room with the smells of perfume and hair lacquer and the sounds of breathing and snoring. They popped up and found themselves on a nice soft rug. There was a wide and tall object in their way, but mice are good climbers, so they scrambled up and on to something even softer and warmer than the rug. It was their first time ever on a bed and they enjoyed the feeling very much. So much, in fact, that they didn't want to leave it. But they were hungry, so they raced across the bed and its slumbering occupants. When they skidded down Frau Streicher's face (she'd smeared it with cold cream, as per her bedtime beauty routine), the terrified woman woke with such a deafening cry that her husband leaped up and tumbled to the floor.

At first, he thought a bomb must have fallen on their building. He quickly felt his arms and legs, but they were all still intact. He scrambled to his feet and flicked the switch on the wall. The overhead light came on and B and B were caught in its glare. They panicked, not knowing which way to go. It was their worst nightmare. And it had all been going so well till then.

'Kill them!' Frau Streicher screeched.

'Yes, yes!' Her husband stood beside the bed, stock-still, staring down at the tiny, surprisingly white animals. 'But how? With what?'

Just then Rolf rushed in. 'What on earth …?'

His mother pointed with an expression of dread at the little lumps of white fur now darting back and forth along the far wall, frantically searching for an exit. 'Quick,' she shrieked, 'the broom!'

Rolf hurried into the hallway, flung open the broom cupboard and fumbled about, knocking over the mop and bucket. He found the required instrument of destruction and grabbed it. Raising it above his head like a Swastika flag in a military parade, he charged back to his parents' bedroom with a bloodcurdling battle cry and began whacking the floor.

But the mice had already fled.

Frau Streicher was sitting on the bed, her slippery face in her hands. 'Kurt,' she moaned, 'I can't take much more of this.' She added with an indignant wail: 'Look, they've peed all over the floor!'

Kurt Streicher laid a comforting hand on Frida's shoulder. 'There, there, my liebling,' he murmured quietly (though he was seething inside). 'We'll get them in the end. I promise you that.' But he had no idea how.

'It's too humiliating!' declared Rolf. 'We Germans are the master race, are we not? Yet we keep allowing those miserable rodents to invade our home.' With a loud huff, he slouched off to his bedroom, dragging the broom behind him. As he passed a nervous-looking Schatzi, who had taken shelter under the hall table during the uproar, he snarled at her. 'And *you* stay out of my way, you useless mouser!'

Following this second scary event, B and B had to reconsider their tactics. Quite simply, they could no longer risk entering that dangerous territory again … at least not on their own. They agreed that they would only visit the Streicher apartment en masse, with their comrades and allies, the house mice. It would be nothing short of total war. But that called for careful planning, so they would bide their time.

Things quietened down at the Streicher home after that harrowing nocturnal event, much to the family's relief. They assumed that the hateful mouse intruders had finally been scared off by their noisy rage. The Polish forced labourer had been brought in again and made to scrub the whole apartment until it sparkled. Then they waited and waited … and no mice.

So at last the Streichers could begin to plan the big dinner party. There was a lot riding on it. If all went well and the high-ups were suitably impressed, it would definitely ease Kurt's way up the career ladder at the Reich Security Main Office. What he was angling for – and his equally ambitious wife was eager for it too – was his promotion from *Kriminal Inspektor* to the higher-ranking *Kriminal Kommissar*. He savoured the very sound of the word *Kommissar*. It sounded so commanding.

'What should we serve our guests at the dinner, liebling?' he asked Frida as they sat together one evening, the uplifting strains of a Wagner opera emanating from the radio.

She glanced up from her magazine, the Adolf-approved *National Socialist Women's Monitor*. She'd been reading an article about the importance to the Reich of women bearing a lot of children – four or five was a good number, according to the article – and once again was made to feel inadequate by having an only child. After Rolf was born her doctor had told her she could have no more babies, for medical reasons. And she had to explain this every time someone asked her why Rolf had no siblings. It had become so tedious of late. She knew it was a black mark against her and her husband, so she tried hard to make up for it with her zealous pro-Nazi views.

'Sorry, Kurt, what did you say?'

'Shall we think about the menu for the dinner party? It needs to be very special, as we must impress our guests. Let's plan it all now, then we can invite them.'

'Yes, of course.' She considered the matter. 'We'll need to use the black market for some items, you know.'

Kurt nodded. 'I'll pull some strings.'

'The main course should be properly German. Traditional.'

'Absolutely!'

'Roast pork, roast potatoes, bread dumplings, sauerkraut and green beans.'

Kurt smiled broadly. 'My mouth is watering already.'

'And for dessert, another of our German specialities: Black Forest cake.'

'Excellent choice. In Berlin everybody loves it. We'll get the bakery to add extra cherries and whipped cream.'

Frida nodded her approval. 'But to start the meal, let's be adventurous and go French.'

'What do you have in mind?'

'Goose liver pâté. They call it *foie gras*.'

'Ha! That should make them sit up and take note.' But Kurt was already pondering on how he would obtain the exotic pâté.

'And to drink with it, the finest French champagne.'

'Yes, let's jolly them along with bubbles. They will be so merry, I wouldn't be surprised if they name me the next Chancellor of the Reich!' He chortled, but Frida shot him a stern look, so he stopped at once. 'A joke, liebling.'

'And finally, to end the meal, let's offer the men cigars with their brandy.'

'Certainly. You think of everything, Frida. I wouldn't know what to do without you.'

'True. And don't you forget it.' She grinned, ever so slightly, and went back to reading her magazine with a satisfied air.

The guest list was finalised. Top of the list was his boss, *Kriminal Direktor* Heinrich Deutsch, and his formidable wife, Hannelore. Then came his best buddy in the SS, Karl Schlepper – always a reliable man and so good-natured – and his wife, the delightfully flirtatious Susi. And finally, the SD intelligence officer Friedrich Frank. He was a secretive character who seemed to wield a lot of power within the security services, so it was a good idea to be in his favour. He was unmarried but would no doubt bring as his date one of the stylish women he sometimes escorted around town.

Although the mice problem seemed to have abated at last, Kurt Streicher was taking no chances. In the lead-up to the dinner party he intended to bring the Polish woman back to stand guard at night, to make sure there were no more invasions from the blasted gnawers. To be sure of her compliance, he and Frida resolved to treat her nicely and call her by her name instead of the customary *Hey you*. Her name was Kasia. (They didn't bother with her Polish surname, as they couldn't pronounce it.)

'Listen, Kasia,' Streicher began to explain slowly, as if talking to a child. 'You are to sit directly outside the larder door. And mind you don't fall asleep or those mice will sneak around you, get into the food supplies and cause mayhem. And we can't have that because this dinner party is a significant occasion. Do you understand?'

'Yes, sir.'

'Very good. Now, I believe you're from the countryside, right? A farming family?'

'Yes, sir.'

'So you're used to seeing mice around and aren't frightened of them, am I right?'

Kasia nodded.

'I presume you know what to do with them when you see them.'

'Oh yes, sir.'

He looked at her earnestly. 'And what is that?'

'Well, sir, I would catch them and dispose of them.'

'Mice can run very fast, and they're cunning. How would you catch them?'

'Sir, my father once showed me an effective method.' Kasia's demeanour of humble servitude now changed and she grew more lively as she related the tale. 'He was most inventive, my father. And he too was plagued by a horde of mice on the farm. So one day, he half-filled a bucket of water and across the top of it, suspended from a rope, he hung a tin can smeared with jam. He leaned a plank against the bucket, to act as a ramp. That night when the mice came, they were attracted to the jam, climbed up the ramp and along the rope on to the can, but as the can spun around, the mice fell into the bucket and drowned.'

'Ingenious! When you next see your father, you must congratulate him from me.'

'My father is dead, sir. German soldiers shot him shortly after they occupied Poland.'

'I see. That's a shame. What was your father's crime?'

'He tried to stop the soldiers from taking our only pig.'

After a pause, Streicher said simply: 'Hmm. War isn't a pretty thing, Kasia. But one day we will have peace again. So the sooner the great German Reich wins this war the better.'

But Kasia didn't agree with that last statement. She didn't agree at all. And if she could have her way, it would be the Streichers drowning in a bucket instead of the mice. It had been bad enough working twelve-hour days on meagre rations at the steaming laundry, washing the shirts and bedsheets of the despised enemy. But at least at the laundry she didn't have to make polite conversation with them.

She decided then and there that if the rodents turned up and threatened to spoil the Streichers' dinner party, she would do nothing to stop them. In fact, she might even welcome them in.

Chapter Ten

AN AUDACIOUS RAID RUINS EVERYTHING

To the Streichers' delight, all the guests on the list
accepted the dinner invitation. Now they set about
sourcing the fine foodstuffs required for the meal.
Rationing and the limits of state-issued food stamps
would pose no difficulties for them, because well-
connected employees of the Reich Security Main
Office could always circumvent the rules that applied to
ordinary folk. The extra-special item on the menu,
goose liver pâté, was made in France and very
expensive. Kurt Streicher smiled to himself to think
that one of the best things about Germany's occupation
of France was the easy access it gave chaps like him to
such Gallic goodies.

Of course, there were harsh penalties for using the black market, the illegal trade in hard-to-obtain items – at the least, a good beating and a prison sentence. But the Gestapo cared not a jot about breaking laws. They'd been given to understand that they were above the law, free to act as they saw fit. Kurt Streicher's contacts were only too willing to supply him with the pâté, plus three bottles of champagne.

Kasia was given her instructions for the evening, which included serving food at the dining table, keeping the guests' drinks topped up, and washing up afterwards. Frau Streicher managed to rustle up a maid's uniform for her – a black dress with a frilly white apron and cap – through her social circle of well-heeled Nazi ladies. When Kasia tried it on in front of a mirror she groaned at the sight. The final humiliation!

The night before the dinner party Kasia set the bucket trap, as she'd been ordered, but in the morning it was empty of mice. 'This is a very good sign!' exclaimed Kurt Streicher. 'But stay on your guard,

Kasia.' And on the basis that there was no harm in making the occasional threat, he added: 'If you know what's good for you.'

When Frida returned, freshly coiffed from the hairdresser's, she busied about in the kitchen preparing the dinner and giving orders to the uniformed Kasia. 'Tidy your hair, girl,' she snapped. 'You're not on a farm now. There are prominent persons coming this evening, as you know.'

Later, Frida put on her best silk dress – slinky and navy blue with a pretty lace collar – and admired herself in the mirror. With her face expertly made up (that new shade of red lipstick was divine), she would undoubtedly charm Kurt's boss. His promotion, she mused, was practically in the bag already. *Kriminal Kommissar Streicher and his wife, Frau Kommissar Frida*, she chuckled to herself.

The wonderful mingled aromas were beginning to flow out of the kitchen and permeate the apartment. Succulent pork with a rich gravy seasoned with parsley, rosemary and thyme, roast onions and potatoes and steaming sauerkraut flavoured with caraway seeds. Kasia had never seen such a feast.

In due course the guests arrived and were seated in the drawing-room, handed glasses of champagne and offered dainty hors d'oeuvres of goose liver pâté on thin slices of toast. It was all highly sophisticated. Everyone was impressed. And it took a lot to impress Kurt's boss, Heinrich. He was used to the best. He had travelled to many of the Nazi-occupied countries and was well acquainted with their cuisines and delicacies. Belgium, Holland, Denmark, Yugoslavia. (Although naturally he was in no doubt that German fare was superior.) He smiled benignly at his wife, Hannelore, as she stuffed another hors d'oeuvre in her mouth and nodded her approval.

Kurt's SS pal Karl chatted mockingly about the 'stupid Russian peasants' the Germans were fighting on the Eastern Front and laughed loudly at his own jokes. His wife, Susi, was sitting pertly on the edge of a chair, showing off her shapely legs and giggling. *She's a little empty-headed*, thought Kurt, *but really quite fetching*. Still, mustn't flirt tonight – the boss wouldn't like it.

The inscrutable intelligence officer Friedrich had arrived last, together with a woman none of them had seen before. She was Mediterranean-looking, with her dark hair and dark eyes, and Friedrich said she was Italian and worked at her country's embassy. Her name was Sofia. She spoke very little, and when she did it was with a strong accent. Ever the perfect hostess, Frida did her best to engage her in pleasant conversation, but to herself she thought: *I know a spy when I see one. Just what is she up to in Berlin, I wonder?*

Schatzi had been the centre of attention for a while – a glossy-furred cat with a noble background tends to be universally admired. But barred from her favourite chair (now occupied by Susi), she quickly tired of the fawning humans and sashayed off for a snooze on the Streichers' comfortable big bed.

Meanwhile, in the kitchen, Kasia was putting her crafty plan into action. She knew from past experience that mice were especially attracted to certain aromas, and chief among them was the smell of sizzling bacon. With the dinner all ready and laid out on the kitchen table, she proceeded to fry the bacon. Soon its enticing scent permeated the kitchen and mingled with the delicious aroma of well-seasoned roast pork. This splendid olfactory invitation wafted through the cracks and gaps in the walls and floors, and it didn't take long to reach the lair of B and B and their gang of house mice, whose quivering whiskers immediately alerted them to the extra-special culinary doings nearby.

They began squeaking and cheeping excitedly to each other, and their sing-song messages all came to the same conclusion: *This is the moment to strike.* So B and B gathered their forces – as they knew, there was safety in numbers – and moved in. Through the gaps and crevices they swarmed, a good two dozen strong, avoiding the guest-filled drawing room and heading for the hallway and kitchen.

The sight that greeted them was without doubt the most magnificent they had ever seen. There may have been a war on, with untold millions around the world suffering grave hardships, but as far as these

Berlin mice were concerned, they'd never had it so good.

They were aware that a human was present, leaning silently against one wall of the kitchen, but their sophisticated *Mus musculus* communications system told them that this particular human was no threat. So, without further ado, they tucked into the feast before them – some into the meat and some into the veg, while the sweet-toothed ones headed straight for the rich, cream-topped Black Forest cake.

Not far away, a slumbering Schatzi woke up with a start. Even a fat and lazy cat can sense when there is something dodgy afoot. She leaped off the bed and followed her nose, prowling towards the kitchen. When she got there and saw the maddening army of mice and the chaos they were creating, she growled in fury, hissed and spat and arched her back. For a moment she didn't know which one to chase first – there were so many of them. Then she sprang into action and started chasing all of them at once, jumping up and down from floor to table and back again, from chair to chair, all over the food-filled bowls and platters, and in the process knocking them over and making a horrible din. The mice, their mouths full of delectable morsels, fled all around the kitchen as they evaded Schatzi's sharp teeth and claws.

As for Kasia, she continued to lean against the wall, arms folded, surveying the scene with quiet satisfaction.

All of a sudden Frida Streicher burst into the kitchen, angrily demanding to know what the commotion was about. At first, she could barely take in the sight of the cat-and-mouse battle that was demolishing the meal she'd been about to serve her guests. When she got over the shock, she screamed. Her husband came rushing in, closely followed by the curious guests.

Susi squealed in horror as a mouse ran between her feet. Her husband Karl's good humour completely deserted him and he just stood there, staring open-mouthed at the pandemonium. The sultry Sofia called out something in Italian, grabbed hold of Friedrich's arm and the pair marched out of the apartment without another word. When Kurt saw his boss's eyes flash towards him darkly, his heart sank. 'Well well, Kurt, this is a bad business,' Heinrich muttered. 'A very bad business.' Then he turned to his wife, Hannelore, the only one who seemed unperturbed by the whole shocking affair (which made her seem all the more intimidating), and said, 'Come along, dear, let's go home.'

Kurt Streicher was in no doubt that this disaster spelled the end of his dream of promotion. How could he be a *Kriminal Kommissar*, ruthlessly chasing down enemies of the state, when he couldn't even keep mice from overrunning his home? The dinner that was meant to be a shining success had turned into a most embarrassing shambles, and would never be forgotten or forgiven.

By now the mice had all fled and Schatzi was lying exhausted under the kitchen table, looking defeated, having caught not a single mouse. It had all been too much for her. Kasia was still standing there, casually, and it was obvious to the Streichers that she had deliberately let this catastrophe happen. So much for her father's failproof bucket trap.

'You!' Frida yelled. 'You did this on purpose!'

Kurt approached the young Polish woman menacingly. 'Don't think that your treacherous actions here will go unpunished,' he hissed. 'You will regret collaborating with the rodents.' He led her away by the arm, pushed her into a closet and locked the door. Then he called the police and had her arrested.

Kasia spent that night in a dank police cell. She knew she was in for a hard time. But as she wrapped her worn old cardigan tightly around herself and tried to sleep, she felt it was a price worth paying.

Chapter Eleven

MORE MOUSE MAYHEM

B and B and the gang had enjoyed the thrill of the dinner party raid so much that they decided to return for more merriment. So a few nights later the rodent army headed back to the apartment. When they got there it was very quiet. There was nobody around, and even the cat had vanished. What luck! However, they were astonished to find the larder completely empty. There was nothing. Not a nibble.

Disappointed, they looked around for something else to get their teeth into. Mice love to explore and are bold and venturesome. So with B and B in the lead, they stormed the study and scrambled on to the antique desk. Its hinged worktop was open and piled with folders stuffed with papers. Paper wasn't nearly as tasty as peanuts or Black Forest cake, but it was just as useful in keeping the teeth sharp, so the mice brigade chomped their way through the folders.

Once they had destroyed Kurt Streicher's files on the fugitives he was hunting – not only with their gnawing but by peeing all over them, so that no one would ever want to handle them again – they scooted off to engage in another favourite mouse pastime. This was the chewing of electric wires. As in any well-appointed home, there was wiring everywhere, behind the walls and above the ceilings. It didn't take long to get to it. And there was no one to interfere with their fun. By the time they'd finished working on the wires, the apartment's electricity supply had been well and truly short-circuited. Of course, the mice didn't know or care about electricity, they just enjoyed the chewiness.

After this latest escapade, the mice returned to their lair for a well-deserved rest. They all agreed it had been a good night, although it was a shame about the empty larder. But if they had to hunt elsewhere for their nosh, so be it. They were *Mus musculus*, wily and resilient, with a long history of survival behind them. They would be just fine, they assured each other. And so they snuggled down for a long kip: Benny and Bobby, the two snow-white lab mice, and their allies, the mousy-coloured house mice. For the time being at least, all was well in their hidden world.

After their traumatic dinner party, the Streichers had left Berlin to spend the weekend recovering at Frida's parents' home in a village south of the city. Frida was in a state of nervous tension and Kurt was quietly morose. Rolf didn't want to be there at all, as he was bored by village life and suspected his grandparents of being less than enthusiastic about Adolf and his new world order. But the elderly pair weren't stupid. They chose their words carefully in front of Rolf, as Hitler Youth boys had been known to denounce family members to the Gestapo – and in front of Kurt, who *was* the Gestapo. They reckoned it was best to keep shtum about everything, except maybe the weather.

Frida decided that she'd had enough of Schatzi, whose feeble attempts at mouse-catching had ended in such dire failure. There would be no more feeding her fine foods, warm milk at breakfast and chicken broth at suppertime. No more grooming her silky fur and granting her pride of place on the best armchair. The puffed-up cat would be returned as soon as possible to the equally snooty Frau Hubermeyer. Until then the cat could just slum it at her parents' rustic cottage, where she would live off scraps and sleep on the wooden floor. Her pampered aristocratic life would be replaced by the austere existence of a humble country moggy. *Let's see how she likes that*, Frida thought.

The Streichers arrived back at their apartment on Sunday night, only to confront yet more trouble: the lights weren't working.

'Really, this is too much!' cried Frida. She threw herself on her bed and sobbed. And that's where she stayed, her hair and clothes awry, until morning.

For her husband, the far greater disaster was the ruin of his crucial Gestapo files. This would set him back weeks, if not months. Some of the criminals he'd been hunting might now never be caught, and that included the Resistance members who had helped the Baums get away. His reputation at the Reich Security Main Office would surely be in tatters after this. Almost overnight, everything had gone catastrophically wrong for him. And all because … he could hardly bring himself to admit it … all because of some foul and devious *mice*!

The idea suddenly occurred to him that perhaps the whole mouse invasion had been a dastardly plot by British spies, under the orders of their Prime Minister, Winston Churchill. Yes, that had to be it. He should inform his superiors at once.

'They will think you've lost your mind, Kurt,' said an exasperated Frida. 'And I would agree with them. Spying mice indeed.'

Not long after this, the Streicher family moved out of the five-storey building near the Tiergarten park in central Berlin. They found another apartment, on the outskirts of the city, which had become available following another arrest of 'enemies of the state'.

The Baums' old apartment, now notorious in the neighbourhood for 'the night of the mouse army invasion', remained empty for months. Then in 1943, the Brits began their serious bombing raids on Berlin. Mosquito fast bombers and heavy, droning Lancaster bombers flew overhead in great waves and pummelled the city.

The tide of the war had turned and the Germans no longer looked unbeatable. They had been defeated by the British in North Africa at the Battle of El Alamein, and by the Russians at Stalingrad. The British and Americans had landed in Italy, and Italian dictator Mussolini, Adolf's staunch ally, had been toppled from power. The world was slowly closing in on the Nazis. Most humiliating for Adolf was the gradual destruction of his once proud and stately capital city. Grand buildings, factories, department stores, elegant old cafes and residential houses were turned into piles of rubble.

Over the next two years the bombs kept dropping, until finally, in the spring of 1945, the long war against Adolf and his evil empire was won. When the dust had settled, Germany's great cities lay in ruins.

At his underground bunker in Berlin, Adolf was dead. His henchmen had fled or been captured. The Russians had taken over and they were very angry. Now that the tables were turned, they wanted revenge, so it was still dangerous for the people of Berlin.

That summer, a small number of Berliners started drifting back to their old neighbourhoods in search of their former homes and the loved ones they'd been separated from. But they found it hard to recognise the streets where they had lived; often there was barely a building left standing, and they struggled to find their relatives and friends.

These were the survivors. Against great odds, they had outlived the concentration camps, brutal interrogations, imprisonment and forced labour, or a perilous existence in hiding or under a false identity. Among them was Dr Josef Baum, who was searching for his wife and son.

Chapter Twelve

REUNION IN THE RUINS

After his years living under a fictitious identity as the widowed schoolteacher Hermann Winkler, it felt strange to Dr Baum to be back in Berlin as himself. For so long he had feared being betrayed or exposed as a fugitive. Now, as he walked the ruined streets, everything seemed unreal to him. Berlin looked like the landscape of another planet.

With some difficulty he eventually located his old street and the apartment building where his family once had their home. It had been so badly bombed, with collapsed ceilings and walls blown out, he couldn't imagine anyone still lived there. He stood in front of it for a while and stared, utterly dejected. So, everything they had was gone. As he was about to walk away, to his amazement the front door opened and the building's elderly caretaker, Herr Stuber, whom Dr Baum knew well, emerged carrying a bucket. The two men looked at each other with incredulity. Then Herr Stuber hurried over and shook the doctor's hand.

Dr Baum learned that while the residents had been forced to abandon the building as the bombing worsened, Herr Stuber managed to remain in the cellar, where he was relatively safe. No electricity, gas or running water, but then there wasn't much of those anywhere else in Berlin by the war's end.

The caretaker said he hadn't seen Mrs Baum or their boy, David. He knew nothing of their whereabouts or whether … he couldn't bring himself to say 'whether they are even alive'. But he could answer the doctor's questions about the family that had lived in the Baums' apartment after their abrupt departure.

'They were called Streicher, Herr Doktor, and I was wary of them because I believe the man was in the Gestapo. He was always prying. Wanted to know everything about all the residents. And, of course, he was most curious about you and your whereabouts. But I knew nothing about where you had gone, so I could tell him nothing.' Then he quickly added: 'Not that I would have revealed anything in any case, Herr Doktor. And this Streicher had a son, a Hitler Youth boy, who was just as alarming as his father. Morning, noon and night he would give the *Heil Hitler* salute to all and sundry.' Herr Stuber shuddered at the memory.

'Was everything in the apartment destroyed in the bombing? Is it possible to go up and look around?'

'Look around? Oh my goodness no, Herr Doktor. It is far too unsafe. There are barely any floorboards still intact to walk on.'

Dr Baum let out a deep sigh.

'They threw out your fine old books, I'm afraid.' Then Herr Stuber clicked his fingers. 'Ah, I almost forgot. There is one piece of good news. When the Streichers moved out – they were having problems with mice and announced one day that they'd had enough of the "invaders" – they took some of your furniture with them. Who knows, you might be able to claim the items back? The Gestapo is kaput now!' He threw his head back and laughed.

'Do you remember which items they took, Herr Stuber?'

'Hmm. Let me think.' After a pause he replied: 'I can only remember one – the beautiful secretaire desk. It was in two parts and took a lot of careful hauling down the staircase.' He chuckled. 'I can still hear Herr Streicher yelling at the removal men: "Be careful with that, you idiots! It's an antique!"'

Dr Baum smiled and touched the caretaker's arm. 'And would you happen to have the address they moved to, Herr Stuber?'

'I would. Let me go back to the cellar and find it for you.'

A few minutes later he returned and handed the doctor a slip of paper. 'Good luck to you, Herr Doktor.'

'Thank you, old friend.' They shook hands again. 'If my wife and son turn up here, please tell them I'm looking for them. There will be an office somewhere in the city for registering survivors. We must go there to find each other.'

'Certainly, Herr Doktor.'

Dr Baum made to leave, but then, hesitating briefly, turned back to Herr Stuber. 'Mice, you say? Well. How interesting.'

The great 19th-century New Synagogue in the centre of Berlin – once so magnificent – was a burned-out shell. But the building next door, which had also belonged to the Jewish community, luckily survived the war intact. And it became a meeting place for surviving Jews. When Dr Baum arrived, he was met by a milling crowd packed into two downstairs rooms. There were men and women, many of them thin and sickly, and youngsters who seemed lost and confused. Stuck on the walls were lists of names. These were the members of the community who had made their way back to Berlin, or had managed to survive by hiding in the city during the war. Other records were being compiled too, naming the victims, the ones who would never return.

Dr Baum squeezed his way through the crowd towards the lists and began to read. After a while an official with a clipboard approached and asked his name, which he wrote down before moving on.

On the opposite side of the room a woman with greying hair was also reading names on a wall. She wore glasses and had to stand quite close – years of grinding work as a housekeeper, cleaner and cook had aged her considerably. She had been coming here every day for two weeks, but had not yet found the names she was looking for. Disappointed once again, she moved towards the exit, scanning the faces of the people around her.

She paused in the open doorway. Outside it was warm and sunny. The city was mostly in ruins but she could sense it coming back to life. There were cyclists pedalling by, old people carrying meagre bags of provisions, children playing in groups on the street, young mothers pushing prams, an occasional businessman striding along with a briefcase. Here and there a cafe or shop, although damaged, had reopened. There were very few cars, but some of the trams were running again. Hope was returning. But where was her family?

When they'd split up three years earlier, it was considered safer for them, and for their rescuers, not to know one another's exact locations. No doubt it was the right decision at the time. But it made it harder for them to trace each other now. This meeting place was their best chance.

From the open doorway she turned back into the room and searched among the mass of people until she spotted the man with the clipboard. She approached him and took hold of his arm.

'Sir,' she said, 'please take one more look at those names you have written down there.' She tapped the clipboard with a finger.

He was exhausted and sweating from all the pleading and enquiring, as well as from the summer heat. 'Name?' he asked.

'Baum.'

'Baum, Baum, Baum,' he muttered as he skimmed through the names he'd been jotting down on the smudgy pages of his clipboard. He stopped and raised his eyes. 'First name Josef?'

'Yes!'

'*Dr* Josef Baum?'

'Yes, that's my husband!'

'Mrs Baum, I saw your husband right there,' and he pointed to the far wall, 'about ten minutes ago.' He grinned at her as he wiped his brow. 'So you are both alive and well,' he said, before proclaiming 'Mazel tov!' (which is Jewish for 'congratulations').

Hannah pushed her way excitedly through the throng until she saw the back of a head she recognised, though the hair was thinner. 'Josef,' she said in a low, choked voice. Her husband turned round. For several minutes the couple could do nothing but stand there and embrace, sob with relief and repeat each other's name.

Then Dr Baum whispered, 'Let's find our son, Hannah. Let's find our David.'

Chapter Thirteen

A WELCOME RIDE IN A JEEP

Captain Solly Stern of the US Army's 2nd Armoured Division was in high spirits as he sat beside the driver in his jeep. After three years of combat – in North Africa, Italy, France and finally on the enemy's home turf of Germany – this division was the most battle-hardened of the war. Its battalions of relentless, rumbling Sherman tanks had earned it the nickname 'Hell on Wheels'. Now, with the war won, it had been awarded the distinction of proceeding straight into the heart of Adolf's vanquished empire, Berlin, to be stationed in the city's American zone of occupation. What's more, they would be arriving on his country's greatest national holiday – Independence Day, the 4th of July.

114

All this meant a great deal to Captain Stern. He was not only an American soldier, but a Jewish one. So, the defeat of a criminal regime that had caused untold death and suffering among his fellow Jews felt personal to him. Entering Berlin as part of a victorious army was a moment he knew he would remember as long as he lived. When he finally got back home to Brooklyn, New York, he would tell his folks about it.

Whistling as they drove through the German countryside at the head of his unit, truckloads of troops behind him, he offered his driver a stick of chewing gum, took one for himself, then leaned back and enjoyed the sunshine.

They were about thirty miles from Berlin, travelling along a tree-lined country road, when they saw a lone figure walking ahead, rucksack on his back. As they drew level, Captain Stern ordered his driver to stop, and held up his hand to halt the vehicles following behind. He saw that it was a teenaged boy, clearly fatigued.

The boy turned to the officer with a broad grin and saluted. 'Good day, Captain.'

'Where you headed, kid?'

'Berlin, sir.'

Captain Stern eyed him quizzically. 'Were you a Hitler Youth boy?'

The teenager let out a laugh.

'Answer me, kid.'

'No, Captain, I was not in the Hitler Youth. They did not take Jewish boys.'

'A Jew?' Solly Stern stopped chewing his gum for a moment. 'Where've you been? How did you escape?'

'I've been living on a farm with false papers, sir. Cared for by good people. Now I am going home, but there are no trains and no other way to get there except on foot. I've been walking for a long time, sleeping at night in barns or under the sky. But I haven't seen my parents for over three years and want very much to get home and find them.'

The captain nodded. 'Hop in. We're headed for Berlin ourselves. We'll take you there.'

'Oh, thank you, sir!' The boy removed his rucksack, slung it on to the back seat and climbed in beside it.

'What's your name?'

'David Baum.'

'I'm Solomon Stern from Brooklyn. And Jewish, like you.' He grinned. 'Well, whaddaya know!'

'I am honoured, Captain.'

'The honour's mine. You can call me Solly.' And with that the jeep roared off and the combat troops of the 2nd Armoured Division followed suit.

Solly was curious. 'So tell me, David, how come a German farm boy speaks English?'

'I was taken to the farm by a man in the Resistance. He had a friend in a nearby village who visited me. I told him I wished to learn English, so he came sometimes in the evening to teach me and give me English books to read. In the daytime I worked in the fields, ploughing, digging potatoes, baling hay. And at night I studied.'

Solly gave out a low whistle of admiration.
'You should go far, kiddo. Hey, want some gum?'

When they got to Berlin, David was shocked to see the state of his home city. As happy as he was that Adolf and the Nazis had been conquered, he despaired to see the great capital's devastation. But Solly Stern reassured him. 'Don't worry, this city will get rebuilt. You'll see. Now you go and find your people. And if I can do anything to help, get hold of me through army headquarters in the American sector.'

'I'm grateful. And I won't forget you, Captain.' He grabbed his rucksack and stepped out of the jeep. 'Oh, and thank you for the gum. It was … unusual.' He grinned.

'Good luck, David Baum.'

The jeep dropped him off in the *Schöneberg* area, not too far from his old neighbourhood, and he began once more to walk. Another shocking sight greeted him as he neared the Tiergarten Park: the beautiful trees had all gone, there were only bare stumps left. He would learn later that the trees had been cut down and used for fuel by Berliners during the long cold winters. Surely, he reflected mournfully, there was nothing in this world more ghastly than war.

As he walked through the dust and debris along his own street, he knew not to expect much of his apartment building to be standing. It would be a wreck like all the others. And when he got there, it was. But to his surprise, an old man was sitting in a battered chair outside the doorway, reading a newspaper. He looked familiar. Then David remembered who he was – Herr Stuber, the caretaker.

He was overjoyed to learn from Herr Stuber about his father's return to Berlin. But where in this huge, bewildering mess of a city would his father be?

David sat down on the ground beside Herr Stuber's chair, leaned against the dusty wall and closed his eyes, feeling as if he could sleep for days. The caretaker brought him a cup of weak coffee, a slice of bread and a piece of sausage. Then he slumped back into his chair and picked up his newspaper, the *Deutsche Volkszeitung*, which meant 'German People's

Newspaper'. The daily paper had been founded by the city's Soviet administration the previous month.

'Wait a minute,' said Herr Stuber. 'I remember seeing something in here that might help.' He quickly thumbed through the pages, before announcing: 'Here it is. It says that the Rykestrasse Synagogue, miraculously not destroyed by the Nazis or Allied bombing, has reopened and is providing temporary accommodation for Jewish survivors. It's about an hour's walk from here, in the Russian sector. Go there and ask for Erich Nehlhans. It says here he's the new chairman of the Jewish community in Berlin. If anyone can help you, young man, it's him.'

The next morning David was standing outside the building where his mother and father had been recently reunited. He had seen their names on the lists of survivors and an official told him that his parents came there every day, hoping to find him. Today they finally would. He was so excited at the prospect that he was waiting impatiently at the entrance, looking up and down the street.

Eventually, he noticed a middle-aged couple approaching. As they neared, his heart beat faster. David found it hard to recognise the parents he'd last seen as a boy of eleven; he would soon be fifteen. They had all changed, and David was now as tall as his father. 'Papa, Mutti,' he spoke the words softly as they fell into each other's arms. It felt like a miracle.

Chapter Fourteen

A SECRET IS REVEALED

For those with no place to live, the community leaders had organised hostel accommodation in less damaged parts of the city – a temporary solution until the survivors had sorted out their future lives. The Baums were allocated two rooms in a lodging house on the western outskirts near Spandau.

The day after their family reunion, Dr Baum announced to his wife and son: 'Now that we're together again, there is a matter I must attend to. I wonder if David would accompany me to an address a few miles away in Charlottenburg? I believe we can get there on the U-Bahn.'

That evening the two set off, and as they sat side by side on the rattling underground train Dr Baum explained the purpose of their journey: they were going to reclaim something that belonged to them and had been stolen from their former home.

'There was a family living in our apartment, an Officer Streicher of the Gestapo and his wife and son, a fervent Hitler Youth member. They moved out after a few months because they were plagued by mice, apparently.'

'*Mice?*' David said curiously. 'That's odd.'

'I thought so too. Any connection, do you think, with your little pets from the laboratory?'

David smiled wistfully. 'Benny and Bobby. I thought of them often during my years on the farm, Papa. It hurt so much to abandon them, and I hoped they had somehow managed to stay alive.' He paused. 'But I'm not sure they could have led a mouse rebellion!'

They both laughed.

'So what is it we're going to take back?'

'Something small, David, but very important. I hope it's still where I hid it.'

The address on Herr Stuber's slip of paper led them to a shabby three-storey block on a narrow side street. Inside it smelled of cabbage and neglect. Upstairs they located the door with the handwritten nameplate reading *Streicher*. Dr Baum knocked loudly.

A minute later the door was opened by a tired-looking woman with dishevelled hair. She was obviously disappointed to see two strangers standing there. 'Yes? What do you want?'

'Frau Streicher?'

She nodded warily.

'I am Dr Josef Baum, and this is my son, David. I understand that for some time in 1942 your family occupied the apartment we were forced to flee in order to evade deportation. The building's caretaker, Herr Stuber, told me you took my secretaire desk when you moved out.'

'Yes, yes. I suppose you want it back now. Fine, take it. I really don't care.'

She flung the door open and they stepped inside. 'My husband threw away everything he found inside the drawers, so don't expect to get that old junk back.'

Dr Baum saw his desk standing against a sitting room wall. He went over to it and ran his fingers gently over its fine walnut surface. It was dusty. Then he pulled down the hinged desktop, revealing two vertical rows of drawers. He removed the bottom drawer on the right-hand side, reached in and slid back a wooden panel. His fingers felt for a push-button. He winked at his son, who was standing beside him, then pressed the button, and with a click out sprang a secret compartment lined in dark blue velvet. Dr Baum lifted it out gingerly. Lying on the velvet, wrapped in a silk handkerchief, was a diamond-encrusted necklace. It was the family heirloom that would help them start a new life, now that everything else was gone.

David cried out in astonishment and gave his father a jubilant hug. Frida Streicher stood a few feet away, staring at the precious necklace with her mouth wide open, before slumping down into a chair.

Putting the necklace back inside the handkerchief and into his jacket pocket, Dr Baum turned to Frau Streicher. 'We'll be on our way now. Thank you.'

'Wait,' she said. 'Please.' Her features softened. 'I have a bottle of cherry liqueur. I've been saving it to have with my husband, Kurt, but who knows when he'll come home. Maybe never. Stay and have a small glass with me.'

Dr Baum hesitated. 'If you wish.'

The three sat together in the dimming evening light, sipping the sweet drink (although David only took one sip, as it was too syrupy for him). Frida wanted to talk. Her days, she explained, were spent with other German women in a bucket-and-spade work detail, paid a few pence an hour to clear mounds of debris from the streets. It was an exhausting, dirty job. Her evenings were spent alone.

'Kurt was captured by the Russians. I believe they shipped him out to some camp in Siberia. I hear they don't show much mercy to members of the

Gestapo or the SS, or even ordinary soldiers of the Wehrmacht. Well, that's what happens when you lose a war, isn't it?' She gave the Baums a quick, bitter smile.

'And what about your son, Frau Streicher?' asked David.

'Well now, there's a shocking thing. My Rolf was conscripted last year when he turned eighteen. He'd been preparing for war a long time and was glad to be fighting for his country at last. His unit was sent to France. But something happened to him there on the Front. I don't know what … the blood, the killing. Maybe the futility of it all. One night he crawled beneath the barbed wire and made his way to the British lines. He pulled a white handkerchief from his pocket and surrendered. *A deserter*. What was he thinking? The army shoots deserters. The shame of it!'

'Where is he now?'

'In a prisoner of war camp in England. He sent me a letter when the war ended. He wrote: "The book was right, Mama."' Frida Streicher rose and went into another room. She came back holding a book, which she handed to Dr Baum. 'He meant this one. I believe it's yours.'

It was *All Quiet on the Western Front* by Erich Maria Remarque, the book Rolf had years earlier saved from the pile of discards and stashed away in his room.

As they were leaving, Dr Baum had a final question. 'I was informed that you left the apartment quite suddenly because of a problem with mice. What sort of mice were they?'

Frau Streicher gave him a bemused look. 'What *sort*? The horrific, infuriating sort. Is there any other sort? Those mice wrecked Kurt's career. He was sidelined, and his most important cases taken away from him. He could never live down the disgrace of letting an army of rampaging rodents overrun his home and destroy his case files.' With a pained expression she described the raids on their larder, the horror of the ruined VIP dinner party, the attack on their electrical wires, and worst of all, the vital paperwork that was thoroughly chewed up and peed upon.

As he took it all in, David tried not to smirk, but it was quite impossible. 'Did you happen to notice the colour of the mice, Frau Streicher?' he asked.

'Colour? Mouse colour, of course!' After a pause she went on: 'Except for the two white ones. Perhaps they were albinos.' She winced. 'Ugh. I can still picture them, disgusting little things tearing around my kitchen.'

On the ride home, David and his father marvelled at the story they'd heard and couldn't stop joking about it.

'They can't still be alive, Papa. Mice only live a couple of years or so. But my Benny and Bobby were true heroes of the Resistance, and I will always honour them so.'

Dr Baum smiled and nodded. 'They were heroes indeed, David. And they could never have known just how heroic they were.'

With the family reunited and once more in possession of their precious heirloom, Josef Baum was eager to contact his brother in England. Noah must be desperate to hear word of them. Josef had sent him a letter but heard nothing back. Maybe he'd moved house.

Chapter Fifteen

AN OLD FRIEND LOST, A NEW LIFE FOUND

Two days after the Americans entered Berlin –
spearheaded by the 'Hell on Wheels' division – the
Brits arrived too. In the vanguard was the 7th
Armoured Division, the legendary 'Desert Rats' who
helped defeat the Nazis in North Africa before fighting
in Italy, then landing in Normandy on D-Day and
battling onwards into Germany. They occupied a
western section of Berlin, next to the American zone.
Perhaps the British Army could help him contact his
brother, thought Dr Baum. He would set off first thing
in the morning to their HQ to make inquiries.

The next day he was polishing his shoes in
preparation to leave when there was a knock on the

door. Hannah opened it and gasped. Her husband looked up. As the door opened wider, he saw a man standing there in the uniform of a British lieutenant. He was smiling broadly.

'Noah!' exclaimed Josef Baum.

'Sorry to drop in on you unexpectedly!' he said. He kissed the flabbergasted Hannah on both cheeks before hurrying over to embrace his brother. David came in from the adjoining room and gazed at the scene, momentarily not comprehending what he was seeing.

'David!' cried Noah. 'You've grown into a man!'

He had brought a tin of real coffee with him (still a luxury in post-war Berlin), and they sat together with cups of the steaming brew, hearing about each other's lives during the six years of the war. Being German, Noah was at first labelled an 'enemy alien' and spent a period in an internment camp. 'But eventually I convinced the British authorities that, as a Jew who'd left Germany to escape the Nazis, I was hardly the enemy, and that I'd be more useful to them as an army interpreter than an internee. So they gave me a commission, and here I am. They need German speakers to interrogate Nazis and distinguish between the guilty ones and those who just let the guilty get away with it. I'll be here for a while.'

Noah put his hand on David's shoulder. 'Your cousins will be so excited to see you again.'

'And I can't wait to see Benny and Bobby. How are they, Uncle?'

'Tall, handsome lads like you, only thoroughly English now.'

'When we meet, I'll tell them all about their fearless little namesakes here in Berlin!'

'Oh?' Uncle Noah looked at his nephew with curiosity.

'A story for when we're all together in England,' said David, beaming at his father.

'Then I shall wait.' Turning to David's parents, Noah continued: 'Now that I've tracked you down and found you alive and well, I will get the plan underway.'

'What plan?' asked Josef.

'I want you three to join us in England. We'll get your official papers in order, passports and exit visas. You'll come and live with us at first, in Preston. Our home will be your home until you're settled with work and can afford a place of your own.'

Hannah and Josef exchanged glances. Too emotional to say anything, Hannah's eyes filled with tears. She clasped her brother-in-law's hand and nodded.

'How wonderful that sounds, Noah,' said Josef. 'Thank you.'

David merely shouted 'Hurrah!', flung his arms wide and knocked over his cup of coffee.

There was still a question of great importance to Josef Baum, one that he was determined to answer before leaving Berlin. What had happened to Emil Vogel and his fellow Resistance members, the courageous souls who had supplied his family with false identities and saved their lives? He had to find out.

He had a distant memory of the apartment where he'd met with them, the home of a woman he knew as Anna. If the building was still standing and Anna still lived there, perhaps she could tell him what he needed to know. He set off to find her.

It took him over an hour to reach her neighbourhood. He entered the side street where she had lived during the war, and after a while located the half-remembered apartment complex with the courtyard. To his relief, although some parts were badly damaged, most of it was still standing. On some of the balconies, washing had been hung out to dry, and he heard the voices of children and mothers calling them.

He couldn't recall her apartment number, so he tried a few buzzers, but no one he spoke to knew of a woman called Anna. As he stood in the entrance hall, studying the occupants' names, an elderly man with a walking stick hobbled in and headed towards the staircase.

'Excuse me, sir,' called Josef. 'I'm looking for a woman who lived here years ago. She called herself Anna, but perhaps that was not her real name. Aged about forty-five, dark brown hair and eyes, a pleasant-looking woman who lived alone.'

'Ah, that sounds like Marthe,' said the man. 'A mysterious woman. She left here during the war. I don't know why. She just disappeared one day.' He leaned against the staircase banister and sighed. 'They were such strange times, one never knew what was going on, or who was getting up to what.' He seemed lost in contemplation, but when he noticed Dr Baum's crestfallen expression he perked up and concluded: 'But Marthe came back about a month ago. First floor, turn left, apartment number nine.'

'Thank you!' Josef Baum hurried past him and bounded up the stairs.

He recognised at once the woman who opened the door, although, like his Hannah, she had aged and her hair was now tinged with grey. 'Marthe,' he said softly. '*Anna.*'

She welcomed him into the drawing-room where, years earlier, the members of her Resistance cell had organised the rescue of the Baum family.

'The Gestapo man Kurt Streicher was obsessed with finding out where the three of you had gone,' said Marthe. 'When he moved into your apartment, I think it really incensed him that you had got away. He decided it would be a feather in his cap to track you down and send you all off to a concentration camp. It was personal, you see.'

'And finding us meant first learning who had helped us.'

'Exactly. We knew he was working hard on it and that the net was closing in.' She smiled. 'But we had an informant, a secretary at the Reich Security Main Office, who tipped us off. Then all of a sudden Streicher was taken off the case – we couldn't work out why – and that gave us breathing space, just enough time to disappear, assume new identities and evade arrest. We could join other Resistance cells and carry on with the fight.'

Josef Baum smiled at Marthe and envisaged the 'army of rampaging rodents', described by Frau Streicher, that had curtailed her husband's investigations. He considered relating the extraordinary tale, but decided she probably wouldn't believe it.

'I met Herr Streicher's wife in her current reduced circumstances,' Josef said. 'A true Nazi even now, I suspect. As for our Gestapo man, he's in Russian hands and I have a feeling he's not enjoying himself.'

'A cause for celebration!'

'Wait, Marthe, I must know – what's happened to my dear friend Emil Vogel and the others – Gunther, Peter and the young man who came to us on the evening of our escape? He never told us his name.'

'I'm sorry, Josef. We all managed to live through the war and contact each other afterwards … all except Emil. There has been no news of him. He was last seen in the final months of the war, when his Resistance cell was infiltrated by an informer. We fear he didn't make it.'

'Betrayed?'

Marthe nodded and looked down at the floor. 'By then the Nazis realised they were running out of time, they were about to lose the war, so they executed their opponents as quickly as they could. It appears they got Emil too. But not before he had saved dozens, perhaps hundreds, of innocent lives.'

Dr Baum put his head in his hands. 'I grieve for him. And I'll never forget the debt I owe him, and all of you.'

As he was leaving, he took Marthe's hands and held them tenderly. 'I hope to make a new life for my family in England,' he told her. 'If you decide to stay here, I wish you a happy future in the new Berlin that will one day emerge from the wreckage of war.'

As the summer drew to a close, so too did the Baum family's days in Germany. When so much of your life had been spent in a country that did its best to destroy you, naturally you feel no remorse in moving on. That autumn Dr Baum, his wife and their son, in proud possession of their official documents, crossed Germany to Holland, and from there boarded a boat to Harwich, on England's eastern coast.

They stood silently next to each other on deck, their faces whipped by the chilly North Sea wind but their spirits warmed by hope and love. The grim past was behind them. A bright new world beckoned.

EPILOGUE

In England, Josef Baum continued in his profession as
a family doctor. In time, he became as well-liked and
respected by his patients as he had once been in Berlin.
He and Hannah remained in the North of England,
where they felt safe and contented. They found a home
on the outskirts of Bolton, not far from his brother and
his family. Weekends were spent enjoying each other's
company or exploring the surrounding countryside.
And in this way, after many years, they grew old and
their lives came to an end.

David had always wanted to follow his father
into medicine, and when he grew up he trained for
many long years and worked hard, eventually becoming
an esteemed consultant at a big London hospital. Every
once in a while, his professional activities brought him

into contact with medical researchers, and he always asked them whether they experimented on mice. If the answer was yes, he shook his head sadly and pleaded: 'Is there no other way?' The researchers considered him eccentric.

He married his English wife, Alice, and they had a son they named Emil, after the friend who had saved his family from the Nazis, Emil Vogel.

When he finally retired, he and Alice moved to the Sussex countryside, where they still live. Friends and family come to visit. David's cousins Benny and Bobby – who remained like brothers to him – would drive down occasionally from the North to stay, along with their wives, until they grew too old and frail to travel. Two years ago, they passed away, first one, then very quickly the other. It's often like that with twins.

Most welcome of all are David's granddaughters, Hetty and Molly.

He had loved watching them grow from little girls to self-assured young women. They sometimes asked him about his childhood in Berlin, about the terrible war years and his time as a farm boy, when he was separated from his parents and living under the identity of Franz Becker. He told them the story of the two lab mice his father had brought home one day, who became his beloved pets. How he had read all about their species, the *Mus musculus*, learned of their ways and taken them to school to show his classmates. How he taught them to twirl like ballerinas. And how for a while they had kept him company in his desolation, when so much had been taken away from him by Adolf and his Nazi followers.

Then he told Hetty and Molly (more than once, as is the habit of grandparents) what he discovered about those dear pets after the war, when he and his father met the hapless Gestapo wife, Frau Streicher. And the girls' eyes would widen with amazement hearing about B and B's riotous mouse exploits.

'Oh yes,' their grandfather loved to say, 'B and B had a far more adventurous and exciting life than they would have done had they stayed in a cage in a laboratory, being prodded and pestered by scientists. And most importantly, they contributed to a great cause

– the defeat of Adolf's empire. They did their bit. A mouse may seem very small and insignificant, but, girls, you must never underestimate the power of the miniscule.'

For many years after the war, David Baum exchanged letters with a German friend in Berlin. They told each other news of their families and their work, they sent snapshots of children and holidays, they shared their innermost thoughts and feelings. The friend even visited David in London on a few occasions. But in old age, he moved into a care home when his health failed, and the correspondence slowly petered out. His name was Rolf Streicher.

Their friendship happened like this. A few months after the Baum family moved to England, David decided to make contact with Rolf. He knew from Frau Streicher that he was in a prisoner of war camp, and with Uncle Noah's help he traced him to a camp in Kent. Rolf and his fellow German prisoners were working on farms and construction sites in the area. David sent him a letter, explaining who he was.

'You lived for a while in my old apartment,' he wrote, 'where I understand you met my pets, a pair of clever white lab mice with pink noses and ears. I named them after my cousins, Benny and Bobby, who are boys. (Later I discovered the mice were girls, not that it mattered.) I heard from your mother that B and B made things rather difficult for your family, especially after they recruited the other mice in the building. Normally I would apologise for such behaviour but as you know, war is war, and your family and the mice were fighting on opposite sides!'

Rolf replied to the letter: 'Thank you for solving a mystery for me! I finally know who had occupied that cage in my bedroom, which I so callously threw out. I'm glad your little white mice were too fast for me that night when they ran across my parents' bed and shocked the life out of my mother. I wanted to wallop them with the broom. But I can see now that they were only playing their part in the Allied war effort!'

In later letters, Rolf told David that his feelings towards the Nazi cause had changed as the war drew to a close. 'I finally read the Remarque novel I found in your father's study – secretly of course, in bed at night when I was supposed to be asleep. Afterwards I tried to put it out of my mind, but it was too late – the seeds of doubt had been planted. By the time I was sent off to fight, I had little stomach for it. And then came the horror of it all. Watching comrades die, being forced to shoot other young men who were really just like me, except they weren't German. And I was afraid of dying. No big hero at all, as it turned out.'

For Christmas 1946, civilians in Britain were allowed to invite prisoners of war to their homes to celebrate the holiday. Rolf wrote to say how moved he was to share their Christmas meal with the English family at the farm where he had been labouring. 'We attended a beautiful carol service together at the village church. And for my Christmas present, they gave me a warm scarf and a thick pair of gloves. Such kindness towards someone who, only the previous year, was a mortal enemy.'

The following summer Rolf was repatriated to Germany. Before leaving, he wrote to David: 'I know of several former prisoners of war here who have chosen to stay in England, some marrying English girls. I'm tempted to settle here myself. But I feel it's time for me to go home. I must see my poor mother. My father has still not returned from Russia. I am all she has left. I will write to you from Berlin. My dream is to help rebuild the city. I'll let you know how it goes …'

Rolf made a good career out of his love of books, becoming a librarian – eventually chief librarian at one of Berlin's fine libraries. As time passed and the older generation was laid to rest (with Kurt Streicher ending his days in Siberia), he and David became the old ones. And they stayed firm friends through the decades, until the end.

It only remains to say a few words about the fate of those two intrepid lab mice, Benny and Bobby. Their short but eventful lives came to a close in late 1943, when the bombs began dropping on Berlin in earnest. At nearly three years old, they were already elderly in mice terms. And what with the continuous terrifying explosions, the crashing masonry, the fires and the panic everywhere, their little hearts gave out, their whiskers twitched one last time and they expired – Bobby first, then a few minutes later, Benny. They always knew they couldn't live without each other.

But there is something else besides their sophisticated communications system, keen sense of smell, impressive climbing skills, voracious appetites and constant peeing that mice are renowned for. And that is producing offspring. Lots and lots of offspring. A female mouse can get pregnant up to ten times a year. And it isn't long before those new mice begin to have babies of their own, and so on and so forth.

Countless generations on, the descendants of Benny and Bobby are scampering under the floorboards and behind the walls, down in the cellars and up in the attics of the houses and apartment blocks of Berlin. They squeak, chirp, sing little songs and tell each other stories about the world around them. And maybe, just maybe, some of them have inherited B and B's indomitable spirit ... and sense of mischief.

Curiously enough, it is rumoured that every once in a while an especially cheeky little mouse is spotted with a mysterious flash of white on its fur, and eyes that one could say are *almost* pink.

THE END

ABOUT THE AUTHOR

Monica Porter is a journalist and author who was born in Budapest, Hungary. Her family escaped after the 1956 Hungarian Revolution and she grew up in New York before moving to London.

She began her career in the Seventies as a staff writer on the weekly Local Government Chronicle, and turned freelance after the birth of her first son in 1978.

She has written for British newspapers including the Daily Mail (for which she has been penning the weekly column, Missing and Found, since 1999), The Times, Sunday Times, Financial Times, Guardian, Daily Telegraph, Daily Express and London Evening Standard. She has also contributed to numerous magazines, including Reader's Digest, Business Life, Woman's Own, Good Housekeeping and Psychologies.

She is the author of six non-fiction books. Benny and Bobby versus Adolf is her first children's novel. Monica has two sons and four grandchildren, and lives in London. www.monicaporter.co.uk